ACID
ASSET

by

M.H. VESSEUR

Also by M.H. Vesseur

North

CEO Groupie

Die Rich

Tax Me If You Can

Nosedive

Power Play

Allusions

Burning Neil Armstrong

Beloved Stalker

Babyface Junkie

In Snuff Park

Sketches Of A Worldwide Christo And Jeanne-Claude

Narcissist Guru

Territory Game

ACID
ASSET

A Radio Detective

A novel by

M.H. Vesseur

Vibes Publishing

Acid Asset

The East German border, a.k.a. the 'Iron Curtain',
somewhere in the second half of the twentieth century...

One

The way the wind worked its way through the endless pine tree woods reminded the secret service man of the shady nature of the land beyond the gate. A hissing sound started in the distance, outside the reach of the human ear, and approached rapidly through the needle canopy, but always unseen. Even when it came very close and evolved into the oceanic noise of breaking waves, it still remained hidden in the trees and showed no more than a moving shade. It rushed and gulfed, and peaked for a moment — almost as if communist agents were rocking the trees barehanded — and then it faded away again. The wind moved around in a shroud of secrecy that fitted the entire nation out there.

It was funny how standing right at the Iron Curtain turned even the hardest government official into a softie. Captain Rosswell stood there, muscular, wearing a sturdy hat and raincoat, and a mustache of a robustness that made him the envy of actors and dictators, and the target of many women of this era. He was responsible for the exchange of a Soviet spy on this windy day — but at the same time he felt like a regular poet!

But Captain Rosswell's musings about the wind and the secrets of the German Democratic Republic were not to last. One of his colleagues, Henri Washington, looking identical though a bit younger, stood next to him going through some papers.

"Herr Doctor Ernst Zschopau, Chemist, high ranking in the scientific nomenklatura of the GDR, specialized in the development of revolutionary new synthetics," he read from a sheet. "Kicked out for no reason at all."

"For reasons unknown to us," Rosswell corrected him. "We're giving them a soviet master spy, so you can trust our bosses for Dr. Zschopau being well worth the sacrifice."

In the brief silence, the wind spoke, even though the forest edge was on the other side of that strangest of all borders, the Iron Curtain.[1] Behind them were the fields of the farmers, and there were no trees close by. The hissing sound definitely came from the other side, a kilometer away, across this strip of no man's land no one was allowed to tread. Along the Curtain, stretching from Northern Europe all the way to the Black Sea in the south, the strip could be as wide as five kilometers, especially at crossings, but in this remote area it was only half a kilometer. Nevertheless, it was a half kilometer well used. The road passed underneath the red-white painted barrier, carried on for a few meters, then was interrupted by a pit, wide enough to stop any car from driving across, and finally arrived at the fence. Here, the Iron Curtain was indeed all iron, masses of barbed wire curling along a straight line like a seashore. Beyond that was the one kilometer zone where you had to pass — in this order — blocks of concrete meant to stop cars and tanks, streetlights that lit up the whole no man's land every night, a concrete road for the East German patrols, a sandy area where footsteps could be traced easily, full of landmines and watchtowers, and finally, before the woods started, another double fencing of mostly barbed wire, and dogs' kennels.

All this could be seen from this side of the border, because they were standing on the slopes of the hills behind them. Most of the East German zone was down in the valley. The look of it never ceased to amaze Rosswell. Or his assistant Washington, so it appeared.

"It's still the stupidest thing to look at," said Washington. "I mean, I can pinch myself, I can think 'Hey, it's real' a thousand times, I can even hear those dogs bark sometimes, but it doesn't help. It's still like I'm in a movie, looking at a studio setup. Like all this is fake and those trees over there are painted on."

"For all I know they are painted on," grumbled Rosswell. "They're of no use to nobody. No kids play in these woods. No lovers take a stroll. It's just a barrier to scare everybody away from a place where no one will go to anyway. If there were no trees there, no one would notice the difference. Therefore they might just as well not be there at all. So theoretically, they are painted and we are looking at some movie screen."

There. More poetry.

But it was not going to be a very poetic day.

Exactly at the agreed time, cars started to approach from the woods. Suddenly the metallic sounds of the gate on the other side as it opened mingled with the rushing sound of the wind in the trees. A series of cars appeared. They were Trabants, driving fast and followed by a tank.

"What's the rush?" said Washington. "Look, they're driving like maniacs."

"Never try to understand the Russkies," mumbled Rosswell. "Or the East-Germans, for that matter."

Washington went through the papers in a hurry, see if he could pick up something he missed, and to his relief he hadn't.

The cars came to a halt in the middle of the sandy zone, so they were still a couple of hundred meters away. Right before their noses someone — who had been there all along without being seen – opened the gate closest to the West.

A voice from a megaphone sounded.

It was some Russian stuff, but Rosswell responded to it by giving a signal towards one of the cars they had arrived in, all the way from Paris. A man emerged and walked slowly towards Rosswell.

"Go home now, comrade," said Rosswell, "and make little spies."

The man was a square Georgian type with eyebrows that were long enough to be waving in the wind on a day like this, and black eyes that stared at him in an unfriendly way. But he gave Rosswell a smile nonetheless.

"Little spies," he repeated. "Yes. Many. With many Russian women. It's either that or freeze to death."

The spy and Rosswell exchanged a nod of the head and then the spy started walking through the first gate. First he passed the actual border, where the red-white pole blocked the road, and then he moved into that zone of fear, that strip of no man's land that a frightened Communist regime had created to keep their people from running to the free West. It was an efficient strategy, because escaping the German Democratic Republic towards the West was virtually impossible. This was proven by numbers.

It was a lot easier to get out with permission from the government, but that privilege was limited to enemies of the state. Once the state had exhausted all available options to silence such an enemy, the only option left was extradition. Or, like today, a swap.

The Soviet spy walked across the no man's land towards the cars that were standing still in the middle of the zone. A figure broke free from the cars. They could see a man walking towards the Soviet spy.

"Exchange in progress," said Washington.

But Rosswell shook his head. "There's something fishy going on," he grunted. He made a gesture with his hand to the team members standing a couple of meters behind them, around their cars.

All looked through the open gate at the walking men.

The approaching man was wearing a raincoat. The only things visible from this distance were his glasses, flickering in the gray light of this windy, cloudy day, and especially his hair. It stood out as if every individual hair wanted to launch itself from his skull, reaching in the direction the wind was pointing at any given moment. This created the illusion that the hair had a life and a will of its own.

When the two men reached each other, they stood still for a moment.

"Walk on, you fool," whispered Rosswell. His voice sounded

tense, as if the air in his windpipe was squeezed out. His face turned red. A curse sounded, mumbled inside his mouth. Then he said, loud: "Pay attention now."

Suddenly Rosswell yelled: "Follow!" Immediately he started running after the Soviet spy, followed by three team members.

Washington stood there, taken by surprise. Because a moment before his boss had started running, the Soviet spy had grabbed Doctor Zschopau, and a fight had ensued. From the Trabants a group of people emerged.

Then the firing started.

"This is nót according to protocol," said one of the team members who where left behind, standing next to Washington. "We are now officially in a diplomatic incident."

"Screw protocol," said Washington. "As soon as we get the Doctor out, it will be as if nothing happened."

Keeping their heads low, Rosswell and his team ran towards the fighting men. There was one guard standing on the other side of the gate, but he just looked pale and was too afraid to take any action. One of Rosswell's team members took his rifle away from him, just to make sure.

The KGB men were running as well, and they were a lot closer already. It looked as if the West was going to arrive at the scene too late. To make it worse, the Soviet secret police had started to fire. Bullets flew overhead or thumbed in the sand, obviously aimed to miss on purpose, but Rosswell's team threw themselves flat on the road, taking no chances. They started to fire back, carefully avoiding actually hitting somebody. Except Rosswell: he continued on his course, running towards the Soviet spy and Doctor Zschopau, covered by the bullets from his team members.

The Soviet agents were taken aback by this powerful response. What was going on here? Was the Soviet spy acting on an impulse when he attacked the East German scientist? Or had this whole thing been carefully arranged? Either way, they had not expected the West to cross the border without any hesitation and launch a full force counterattack.

But before things could get any more complicated, there was an explosion. Or rather, there was a bang and a lot of smoke. A huge cloud of yellow billowed around the spy and the scientist, hiding them from sight. Rosswell's team looked on stunned, until the scientist suddenly emerged from this thick fog. He was running towards them and when he got there they all retreated as fast as they could.

Behind them the cloud of yellow smoke was blown by the wind towards the Communist secret police, obscuring their vision long enough for Rosswell's team to reach the gate and retreat to the West.

"Ein guter Trick, was?" said the Doctor, sitting in the back of one of the secret service team's black Mercedes Benzs. For the first time since his arrival on the Western side of the Iron Curtain he smiled.

"What was it?" said Washington.

"Just some chemicals I brought with me. A nice little mixture to hide myself in. Comes in handy, wouldn't you say?"

"You're a regular magician," said Rosswell. "You could start your own theater if chemistry doesn't work out. Kids in the free world love magic shows."

Engines roaring, the team of Western government agents was in a hurry to get as far away from the border as possible, and hope for the best.

"The children of my country like magic shows too," said Zschopau.

His voice sounded sad and lonely, and when Rosswell looked to the back of the car he noticed that the Doctor was no longer smiling.

"Of course they do, Doctor," he said.

And then, unexpected, Zschopau burst into laughter as he added: "As long as the magician doesn't do the disappearing act! The government hates it when you do that!"

Decades later,
another time, another place...

Two

The cold did not impress Hitomi Sakamoto. She went about her business, producing the radio show The Boardroom, running from meeting to meeting in the city, in offices and restaurants, walking the pavement and diving into the subway, as if all was normal. She grew up in a part of the world where winters could be a lot colder than in this city, but the taste of the local winter laying ahead stimulated her, and she attacked the days with even more energy than usual — which is really saying something, because the slim, fortyish radio producer was a whirlwind to begin with. To see her bringing even more power to the surface was quite an experience, especially for the men around her.

Men like Don Wozniak, sound engineer to The Boardroom. In stark contrast with the tiny Japanese body of Hitomi, moving vividly and restlessly as if to balance her long black hair, he himself sported a belly and a puffed face. The only attempt at fashioning himself were his hairs: thin black pins, waxed into every direction. He would look at Hitomi whirling around the studio and the offices through his huge Thunderbird puppets' glasses and wonder where she got that energy from.

"You in love, Hitomi?" he might ask, or something down that line, but it would always be fruitless.

Hitomi Sakamoto was not going to share stuff like that with Don anyway. "You know nothing of love, Don Lech Wozniak," she would probably answer. "So don't get any funny ideas."

It wasn't until the snow started falling that Hitomi was awed. Immediately memories of her childhood in Northern Japan came back to her. She came out of the subway and the flakes were there. She was ecstatic, ran into the first store she passed on the way to the WCBN Radio building and bought a bright red, woolen hat. By the time she arrived in the WCBN Radio building, a white layer decorated the bright red.

"There's this successful business man coming home after a horrific voyage from his work, through a blizzard," said Carl Pappas, the bizz jockey, with rattling teeth. A white cloud marked his breath.

He was standing in his office on the seventeenth floor of the WCBN Radio building. The city beyond the large windows was mostly hidden in the falling snow, revealing little more than skyscraper silhouettes and office window lights. "He's stamping his feet, brushing the snow off his shoulders, turning his hat upside down to clean it, and shaking heavily from the cold. His fingers are blue. He's making funny noises, so his wife comes running out of the kitchen and she's, like: 'Are you OK?' Because the man is all shaking and looks very pale and there's even some panic on his face.

"So he says: 'It was terrible! I've been through an ordeal.

My car wouldn't start because everything was frozen up and there was no way to get a cab so I had to take the subway. The heater had broken down, and when I got out I had to walk home being already frozen, through this sudden blizzard. I was cold as a corpse. The blizzard was blowing straight into my face. There was not a soul around. I was all alone. I saw only one car pass me, but when I waved for help they didn't respond. I could not see where I was going because the snow blinded me and I thought I was never going to see the light of day again. I will be cold forever.'

"To which the wife answers: 'I thought you were talking about the blizzard, but now I understand! You are talking about our marriage!'"

Behind Carl, someone applauded.

The bizz jockey turned around and looked at Phil Solo, the WCBN Radio boss, walking in.

"You have a painful sense of humor, Carl," said Phil. "You seem to think all married couples are miserably failing and pouring acid over each other on a daily basis."

"You're married," said Pappas. "You tell me. I'm just a regular guy in love with a beautiful woman."

"You've been in love with her for many years. That counts as a marriage. You know as much about couples as I do. Was that your opening speech for tonight just now?"

"Yeah," said Carl, sitting down in the chair behind his desk. "Just made it up."

"Ah, so you're going to piss off Job Messner again. He wrote some very funny lines for tonight, even a great opening joke, if I remember correctly. Why not use that one?" Phil Solo sat down too, raising his arms in despair. "Saves me another speech full of complaints in the morning from friend Messner."

"Job is fine with the way I do things," said Carl. "He appreciates my improvisational skills. But... are they going to fix the heating in here before The Boardroom starts? Look at the two of us: we're standing here in our parkas as if we were outside. How long is this going to last?"

"They're having serious problems heating this floor," sighed Phil Solo, in a rare moment of openness. "No one has the slightest idea why the problem occurs only on the seventeenth. It was supposed to have been fixed twenty-four hours ago, but they had several serious setbacks. Anyway, we got vulnerable stuff covered with the auxiliary heaters by now, so there'll be no more damage. No reason to worry other than my dealings with the insurance company. They'll be on the lookout for someone to blame."

"And I'll be on the lookout for concentration," growled Carl. "You know me, I like my life warm and sunny. I'm shaking and I'm going to sound ridiculous on radio with my teeth rattling."

"You'll be fine, bizz jockey. The studio is insulated, it won't be as cold as it is in your office. But I'll check and see if there's some heating available there."

As he left the room, Carl yelled after him: "At which point does a laptop freeze? Huh? Thought of that?"

He cursed, watching the white cloud emanating from his mouth.

"Carl Evangelos Pappas, you are a bad boy," said Hitomi Sakamoto, walking into the room.

"Look who we have here. It's the Yeti from Japan," said

Carl. He couldn't take his eyes off all the fur of Hitomi's coat, and the remains of snow on her red hat.

"One of these days you are going to make a mistake and curse on live radio," said Hitomi, "and Solo is finally going to have your head."

"Not after all these years I'm not. And don't bet on Solo yet, he was quite the charmer just n-now..."

"You cold? That'll teach you some modesty, you and your luxury life of stuff and central heating. It will be good for you."

"Sa-ka-mo-to!" a voice barked from the door. Don Wozniak barged in. "Did you do your black magic on the central heater, so our whole floor is freezing up? Admit it! Just the thing for you to harass us with your beloved Japanese winter."

It was true. In recent years, Hitomi had spoken of the beautiful though severe winters in the part of Japan where she lived as a child. It had brought forth beautiful poetry and novels and music, and it was something she cherished in her memory.

"Are you kidding? Don Lech Wozniak, you wouldn't stand a chance in such a winter. You'd be in intensive care before first snowfall. Because you haven't got what it takes."

They stood opposite each other as if both were contemplating a real fight. You know, the kind that's physical and can inflict bodily harm.

"I haven't got what it takes to whát? Go on, admit it, you were going to say 'man'. You were going to say I haven't got what it takes to be a man."

His face was turning red, surrounded by the fur of his parka hood.

"Keep that up, Wozniak," said Hitomi, as she started to walk out of the room. "It will keep your blood pumping and that's just what we need right now."

"Has anyone ever checked whether that Japanese town of hers is really in some arctic place, as she claims, or actually on Hawaii?" Don growled.

"How are your fingers, Don?" said Carl. "Are they blue? Can you operate the console tonight or have you got the shakes? I know I do. If this doesn't get any better, we may have to c-cancel the show."

"I made some provisions," said Don. "Got some auxiliary heating to protect the equipment."

"Got some in the st-studio t-too?"

"Yeah. Don't worry about it. No one's gonna hear your teeth. Come one, let's get out of your cold office."

Three

By the time the pre-recorded voice of WCBN Radio kicked in, opening the new live broadcast of The Boardroom, the heat was becoming oppressive. It radiated from the old mobile device Don Wozniak had placed close to the bizz jockey's chair, filling the air with the smell of baking dust, of old clothes on the radiator.

"It's eleven o'clock. The city is dark, but the fire burns. It burns in the offices. It burns on Wall Street. It burns in the City. It burns on the Bund. It burns in Dubai. It burns in the factories and power plants. And it burns within us. Because we are the business and we all need redemption. This is the hour of delusion and today's truth. This is The Boardroom. Here is your prophet, the buddy and the bodyguard of every CEO, the Don Juan of every business babe. Here is the world's one and only bizz jockey. Here is your BJ: Carl Pappas!"

Carl had been looking on as the face of Don Wozniak behind the studio window became redder and redder, while Hitomi Sakamoto took off her new red hat and wiped her forehead.

They had kicked out the cold, obviously.

The only person around who remained unaffected by the sudden and uneven heat from the auxiliary devices was sitting opposite Carl Pappas at the studio table. A distinguished gentleman in his fifties, with a meticulous suit and the looks of an ageing movie star: still in shape, his skin fresh from a lifetime of not smoking and drinking, all his white hairs combed back in unison.

"Men and women of the business," said Carl, close to his microphone, "welcome to The Boardroom, where just like any other day we ask ourselves: where do we stand? If you know the answer, you may call now. But don't take this lightly; many went before you. Many were mistaken. And are grounded now, in court, in jail or in hell. A few moments from now I will introduce tonight's guest, who is already waiting on the other side of the microphone. And while we wait till our first caller comes in, let me tell you about this business man who travelled home during a blizzard..."

The guest looked at the bizz jockey with a vague smile. It could be the smile of a man who pitied the jockey, or a man who knew how to hide his nerves perfectly.

"I'm Boris," a voice coming from a telephone line said, with a thick Russian accent. "I'm an arms trader, Mr. Pappas."

"I see, arms. Listen, Boris, I'm not an expert when it comes to weapons, so tell me, what's you're favorite weapon?"

"The most profitable one, Mr. Pappas."

"Is that the one that makes the most profit or the one that kills the most people, Boris?"

"The killing is not my business, but I guess you have a point. But what I've been meaning to ask you..."

"Fire away Boris."

"Isn't it time you did a Boardroom on Russian business for a change? I feel a bit left out. Are you against Russia, perhaps?"

"We had a whole Russian week on The Boardroom a couple of years back. But why in the world would I be against Russia, isn't that proof of typical Russian paranoia?"

"For a broadminded man you are sure using a lot of clichés about my country, Mr. Pappas. Why not put your money where your mouth is and put some time in the arms business and the success of Russians in that market. We got a large chunk of worldwide business after all."

The bizz jockey sighed and looked at his guest. The distinguished gentleman raised his eyebrows, and smiled vaguely again.

"If I put the arms business on the table in The Boardroom, it will be to put pressure on you people, Boris," said Carl. "I love Russia, hell, I have a Russian banker, and one of the WCBN Radio owners is Russian. But I don't care what country you are from, or anybody, as long as you have a proper set of rules to do business. Guns are causing more misery in the world than anything else, so I'd like you to come and fight it out. I'm against guns. Are you up to that, Boris?"

"Count me in, bizz jockey."

"Thank you Boris, stay on the line and we'll take your address. Annd... we're back to the table here. Like I told you before the weekend, today we're talking about the synthetic future. Whether that is a robot husband or artificial oxygen, that doesn't matter. The point is: if I use the word 'plastics', you will probably think of pollution, of waste that doesn't degrade to its natural origins in a million years. But in reality we are now on the way to synthetics that dissolve quickly after they've been thrown away. Plastic bags that do not litter entire continents by sticking to bushes, but simply dissolve in the first rain that falls on them. You're tired of your microwave oven? You put it out in the air in your garden and it fades in a few months, leaving nothing but natural components on your lawn. How's that for a future for your kids?"

The distinguished gentleman said: "You're a romantic as well as a visionary, Mr. Pappas."

It didn't occur very often: a guest who spoke before he was properly introduced. But that didn't bother the bizz jockey at all. He appreciated any initiative taken by guests, because that added to the live feel of the radio show. The Boardroom as a concept always worked best when things turned impromptu.

"And here's my guest for tonight. Please allow me to introduce to you business folks William Nightingale, CEO of Bering Chemicals for many, many years. Welcome, William."

"Thank you for having me."

"Am I being too romantic or is there a ring of truth in what I just said about the future?"

"I think you are hitting the nail right on the head," said Nightingale. "I'm not sure if the listeners should take all that too literal, though. A plastic bag that dissolves in the rain, that should be good, I guess. We'll have to come up with another solution for rainy countries of course. Many women would welcome an artificial husband they could order around the house. But the point is that it is all technically possible, now or in the near future. Uh, except for the artificial oxygen, I wouldn't know about that yet."

"I love a guest who is at least as romantic as I am about business opportunities," Carl hollered into the microphone, "and the changes of making this world slightly better." And then he turned to whispering. "Of course, we all would like to know: who's talking? What has Bering Chemicals Inc. done that will convince at least some of the ten million Boardroom listeners?"

Don Wozniak, his wrists resting on the console in the editing room, a dot of whipping cream on one of his thumbs and his upper lip, turned to the chair next to him. "I've never heard of Bering. Have you?"

Hitomi kept a straight face, her eyes fixed on the large table in the studio before her, beyond the glass, and took a deep breath — not too deep, because the whipping cream odor was quite close and not the kind of smell she enjoyed. "The Bering Sea. The Bering Strait. Bering Island. The Bering Glacier. Vitus Bering."

"Yeah. Right. Thanks. They're all named after someone?"

This time Hitomi took a breath that involved some whipping cream aroma moving into her smell-o-sphere, which added to the annoyance of having to listen to an ignorant sound engineer.

Being annoyed with the sound engineer was not that much of a task, since Hitomi enjoyed stress and aggravation. These things revved her up. They got her cooking on the front burners, so to speak. Anyone else would have succumbed to an ulcer years ago, but such energies were transformed by the formidable machine called Hitomi Sakamoto. She was efficient. End of line.

Many times the sound engineer's true nature escaped her, however. Don was not so ignorant of the facts at all. He didn't study the topics of The Boardroom broadcasts like Hitomi did, but he did follow the news, talk to all the editorial staff members every day and even read "The Boardwalk" — the show's agenda — occasionally. So tonight he was just fooling with the producer, pretending the name "Bering" meant nothing to him. Just a bit of banter on the side.

"They're named after Vitus Bering," said Hitomi.

Had she looked at Don, she would have noticed his broad smile.

He liked Hitomi, for her toughness, but also for her predictability. It was never a real problem for him to get her climbing a tree and holler at him.

And while the guest was explaining the history of Bering Chemicals Inc., Hitomi gave Don a summary: "Bering Chemicals was founded in the 19th century. Not because its founder is a descendant of Vitus Bering. Not because they took any raw materials out of the Bering Sea floor. It's actually quite romantic, because the founder was on a fishing trawler on the Bering Sea when he was a young man, and he fell overboard in that arctic water in the middle of the sea. You cannot survive in those temperatures for more than seconds, or minutes at the most. But he was rescued nevertheless, which he took as a sign from above. So when he came back ashore he gave up fishing and went to school again and became a chemist and named his own company Bering as a way to show his gratitude."

"Way to go," said Don. "He made a fortune with a company that didn't bear his name and now nobody knows who he was."

"Someday," said Hitomi, "that fate awaits you too."

Four

It didn't take the bizz jockey long to open fire.

"If you're so clever, William Nightingale, CEO of Bering Chemicals Inc.," said Carl, slightly raising his voice, filtering some of the friendliness and joviality out of his voice, "and if you're such a visionary and so full of optimism about the future of this planet, then how come so much of that toxic *crap* is still pouring out of your factories?"

William Nightingale didn't blink, nor did he pale, nor did his smile vanish. He did raise his left eyebrow though.

"Some of our products are still toxic, I agree," said Nightingale, talking slow, almost as if he was stalling for time to think. "I am not going to deny that. Some plastic bags going to supermarkets all over the world still pollute the landscape. I saw photographs of bushes in Africa, and there were plastic bags all over them, held by the thorns. I saw photographs of beaches. Again, white plastic bags all around."

"There's even supposed to be a floating island[2] of plastics somewhere in the Pacific, people," yelled Carl.

"That's exaggerated," said Nightingale, with more authority now. "There are parts of the ocean where microscopic remains of plastics float under the surface. I'm not saying that's good, but the story of a floating island of plastic is simply not true. And it's also besides the point."

"It's still plastic floating around, William," said Carl. "Did I eat any of that stuff when I devoured my salmon filet tonight?"

"Like I said, it's microscopic. Get me a piece of salmon filet and I'll eat it right now."

"That doesn't prove a thing, William."

"No, I guess not. The point is, we've eliminated eighty-five percent of the toxic products we had in the 1970s, when awareness about pollution was born. Most products we simply abandoned. Others have been revised so they are no longer toxic. We're almost there."

"What's almost, William?"

"Ten, fifteen years at the most."

The bizz jockey applauded.

Hitomi raised her eyebrows, the both of them, and widened her eyes. Don sucked the remaining whipping cream from his thumb.

"Well done, William. Unfortunately... that's not enough if you ask me. Come one, why not give us a solid date? Why not give the world a guarantee? Zero toxic products in ten years?"

"I..."

"Don't tell me you have to talk to your lawyers now, William. You have all the knowledge you need to say yes or no. Or say twenty years, but say something."

The vague smile on the face of the distinguished gentleman sitting opposite of the bizz jockey widened and became a full frontal grin. "All right, Mr. Bizz Jockey, I'm taking your offer. If I can't live up to that ten years from today, I will resign."

At that precise moment, the sound engineer hit a button and a cavalcade of notes from an orchestral horn section filled the studio and the airwaves and the internet. It was loud, and short, but long enough to make listeners sit up straight again.

Well done, thought Phil Solo, looking on from the visitor's lounge beyond the other window. We may well be broadcasting a bit of history right now.

"Thank you, William. You're a good sport. Now before we go into the details of the future of zero pollution synthetics, here's one last question about the history of Bering Chemicals."

As the guest answered "Fire away, Mr. Pappas," Hitomi touched her right earlobe, wondering what this last question could be, as all topics had been dealt with. She didn't even have to check the "Boardwalk" — as the show's list of topics was called among the editorial staff — because she knew there wasn't anything left. It was possible the bizz jockey was throwing something in impromptu because there was time enough. There was enough other material for the rest of the show. She took a deep breath; you simply never knew with the bizz jockey.

"Whatever happened to that famous East German chemist," asked Carl, "who defected to the West and was hired by Bering Chemicals? Has he lived up to the promise he was supposed to be, back in those days?"

Right there, Hitomi held her breath.

It doesn't sound like a question that will provoke turmoil,

she thought, and then she relaxed again.

Don, his usual cool self, twisted his neck to the far left and then to the far right, as if to click some bones, but there wasn't a sound.

William Nightingale was unmoved, but he gave it a good try nonetheless, trying to sound empathic. "Well, Mr. Pappas, you got me there. I'm a little embarrassed not knowing about this. What was that chemist's name again?"

He didn't say a name, thought Hitomi. How peculiar.

"Herr Doctor Ernst Zschopau," said Carl. "Surely you must..."

"I have no idea who that is," said Nightingale, sort of offhand. He sounded uninterested. "It was before my time, you see, that whole thing during the Cold War."

There was a silence.

Don was watching Carl's hand: it moved up only a little bit, looking as if the bizz jockey was waving through the window to the sound booth — but of course he wasn't. It was code language, meaning *hold that tune*.

And it wasn't a superfluous gesture, because the silence was *long* — for live radio. Somewhere between five or ten seconds, which felt like half an hour to Don, Hitomi and Phil, and other members of the editorial staff.

Then Carl said: "Of course you were, William. You were young and innocent. Many listeners of The Boardroom were young and innocent in those days. Then the Berlin Wall fell and we all became a smashing success in business. And we all forgot about it all. Well, if he didn't win a Nobel Prize for something he invented or discovered, I guess there's no point in pursuing the matter, now, is there? It's just that... how come you are unfamiliar with your company's history?"

Then Nightingale said: "Like you said: this Doctor has probably not made a dent in history after he defected from the East. In those days, crossing the border was an achievement all in itself, but now it takes more to make people remember you."

The bizz jockey and his guest exchanged the briefest look, unseen to the others beyond the windows. Neither of them looked away.

Then the hand went down to the table. Don Wozniak pushed a button and a music track started to play, slowly at first, to allow Carl to say a few more words.

"I want to sincerely thank our guest, Mr. William Nightingale of Bering Chemicals Inc. for joining us tonight. We've had a serious talk about the future of pollution, you might say, and I think you've been a good sport. Your name is on the line now and I think personal involvement is a good example for everyone. Here are some messages and then we'll be back, talkin' to some callers. William will be here to answer any question you folks might have!"

And Don made a movement with his fingers, upping the volume. He did that in a choreographed way, to impress Hitomi: after touching the console he let his hand move up in the air, and back to its resting position with a wide circular angle in the air.

"And there you are bizzz jockeeeeeey!" he said, turning to Hitomi, grinning a creamless smile. "Don't you just looove that man?"

"I take it that's rhetorical," said Hitomi, and she walked away.

Five

Winter never caught the *Gulag* unprepared. Its owner, Katharina Yekaterina, or *Katie* to her friends and clients, was always ready. She worked through the spring, summer and autumn in a businesslike manner. She ran the restaurant at the city's river bank in an efficient way and didn't go out of her way to do much extra, walking around as a waitress herself. The food was good, the coffee was good, the service was dependable and she never skipped a shift. The cook was treated well, because a good soup could save the day. So she knew her business, but enough was enough.

Until the season's first snow was announced. She would summon one or two of her male staff and get to work that very day, after closing hours. There was a basement underneath the rectangular building, full of stuff that came in handy. Some of this was carried up the stairs and the tables were rearranged.

The next day, every guest would smile at the new interior of the *Gulag*. This time, one of the first visitors of the day was the bizz jockey, Carl Pappas. His girlfriend dropped him off on her way to her work.

Pappas had been sitting next to her, watching her drive the slipping car through the white city. They kissed goodbye through the window.

"Don't get too cold today, Carl," she said, her hair jumping up in the wind, as if each individual hair wanted to dance with a snowflake, "or I won't have any use for you tonight."

He smiled and walked, but he dared not look back at the car, that swiveled away.

As soon as he had slipped across the parking lot to the door and entered the *Gulag*, he laughed. Katie had been at it again!

And there she was, rushing towards him. "Carl! I have been expecting you. Got a place for you by the fire, you must be freezing like an escaped prisoner in the Russian winter. Follow me."

Pappas smiled and saw no reason to do otherwise. It would spoil Katie's fun. Furthermore she had taken his arm with such a steel grip that he really didn't have much choice.

The force of Katherina was formidable. She was a large woman of Russian descent, in her fifties, her hair bleached, and she could be foulmouthed, if necessary, to take on the wrong kind of audience in her beloved restaurant the *Gulag*. Sometimes people thought, because she was Russian and the place had a Russian name, they could behave any way they pleased.

They were wrong.

Pappas was forced down in one of the large armchairs near the fireplace. Burning logs of fire made snapping sounds. A comfortable heat rushed over him like a blanket.

"My beautiful *Lady of the Night*," said Carl. "Look at you! Beautiful as ever. This Siberian winter does nothing to you.

Nothing. But... don't you think you are overheating this place a little bit?"

"We have goulash," said Katie with pride. "And borscht. You are going to love it, Carl."

"No doubt about that," said Pappas, and he added quickly: "after I've had my coffee."

"You're getting coffee with vodka," said Katie, carrying on in her enthusiastic, but also authoritative way.

Carl looked around him. He smiled again. The whole restaurant had been rearranged. The usual straight lines of rectangular tables and chairs had been abandoned. Now tables were combined so they formed squares, spread across the restaurant like islands. All paintings and plants and other obstructions had been removed from the walls so the unpolished planks became clearly visible again, giving the place back its original log cabin ambiance. There was one Russian flag on the wall in a dark corner, next to a portrait of Stalin.[3] The flag was traditionally placed there in such a fashion that if a guest was offended by the old party leader's face, it could be hidden in a moment. For Katie, recreating a Siberian camp shed was a way of honoring her grandfather who had spent years in prison. It was not to be mistaken for anything else. The second portrait, on the opposite side of the restaurant, was that of Aleksandr Solzhenitsyn,[4] the famous author. The snow helped; it built against the windows from the outside.

To top it all, Katie wore a gray communist worker's outfit from days long gone, a long jacket and thick trousers, all way too comfortable for the incredible, tropical heat that was now ruling in the *Gulag*.

"I see you brought the Gulag Archipelago back to life once again, Katie," said Carl.

"Yeah, isn't it great?" she said, with a big smile.

"It's terrible, Katie," Carl said, with a baritonesque deepness in his voice.

They looked at each other and laughed.

"It's a shame!" yelled Katie, and her high pitch roared across the restaurant.

Then she walked off.

Exactly when she had disappeared into the kitchen, Hitomi Sakamoto entered. It would not have surprised Carl if Hitomi had been waiting outside till Katie was gone, thus saving herself one more encounter with the Russian force. Hitomi was not Katie's greatest fan. Katie, on the other hand, couldn't care less.

"Carl Evangelos Pappas, why are you sitting by a fireplace when the whole place is already heated beyond belief?" said Hitomi, taking off her parka. "Your brain must be melting. Let's sit by the window where the heat is cooled down to the point of reason."

It was actually a relief for Carl to be sitting on the edge of the archipelago of tables, as close to a window as they could be. There the tropical heat was slightly diminished, at least to an acceptable level.

"About next week," Hitomi fired away.

"About coffee," said Carl. "Woman, have you no mercy? A new Ice Age has just begun and you want to get started without coffee?"

"Katherina Yekaterina will be right over with your beloved

black tar, no doubt," snubbed Hitomi.

Carl raised his eyebrows, unaccustomed as he was to her current tone.

"Excuse me," said Hitomi. "I have this huge list of things to go through and I have no time for interruptions from this... woman."

"Let's talk about Bering Chemicals first," said Carl.

Then Katie showed up with the coffee. "Bering," she said, "You want to know about Bering? Ask me."

She served them and she smiled at the bizz jockey. Hitomi looked temporarily out the window to avoid... Well, to avoid.

"That's all right, Katie. I'll ask you as soon I know what to ask."

When Hitomi turned, the waitress was gone. Funny how she looks like a waitress, she thought, and not like an owner.

"What about Bering Chemicals?" she said, looking at Carl's coffee. "Carl Evangelos Pappas, whát are you putting in your coffee? Is that a creamer? Don't you know that clutters up the arteries?"

"It's a good thing you don't know what else is in there," said Carl, grinning.

Hitomi took the coffee and smelled. "Oh no! There's alcohol in there. Are you starting to lose it? That's it. You are starting to lose it. All these years of pressure are finally getting to you."

"Bering Chemicals, Hitomi."

"That's behind us. That was last night."

"I know. Don't you think it was funny?"

"Funny? I don't recall."

"The way William Nightingale denied knowing Doctor

Ernst Zschopau," said Carl. His eyes roamed the room, the incredible red of the Soviet flag, the writer and the dictator facing each other. He felt there was a story in all this, how there was something particularly Cold-Warrish about last night and this morning.

"Oh, that," said Hitomi. "I remember thinking how you asked that question out of the blue. It was nowhere in my information, it had never been discussed. Where did you get that information?"

"My gray cells," said Carl. "I remembered reading about that man in the newspaper when I was very young, I suppose. At first I didn't remember his name, it was just in the back of my mind that a defector from the East joined Bering Chemicals."

"It's silly," said Hitomi. "It was decades ago. Of course Nightingale had no idea. No one has any idea."

Carl sipped from his coffee. It was appropriately awful for a man with a unique approach to coffee. For him, expensive, superior coffee treats were to be saved for special occasions. On an ordinary workday, coffee should be black, thick and old. It was best if it had been standing on a heater for forty-five minutes, to be precise, when it was still fresh enough to pour but at the point of losing the remains of that freshness.

"How can you drink that," Phil Solo often said, when they visited the *Gulag*. "She also serves great cappuccinos, why settle for this?"

"On a workday, coffee is not supposed to be a treat to the tongue," Carl used to reply. "It is meant to give you a shave."

"I don't see how this defected scientist can be an interesting topic," said Hitomi.

"I have a funny feeling about it," said Carl. "From most people I would have accepted a 'no'. But William Nightingale? No way. That man is way too intelligent and well informed. I know his reputation. I've read dozens of interviews. William Nightingale knows éverything."

"So?" said Hitomi.

Her cell phone sounded.

"So he was lying when he said he had never heard of Zschopau."

"Hitomi! Yes. No. I'm with the bizz jockey right now. It will have to wait. No. Wait. We can talk about it at the gym tonight, that'll work faster. Ciao."

Carl smiled. "You are an amazing woman," he said.

"Nightingale was lying? Why would he do that? And how do you know?"

"He looked at me when he was lying. He was challenging me. Unknowing, I suppose, but he was challenging me."

"Bollocks."

"Thank you for being concise, Sakamoto. Trust me, Nightingale is hiding something. Why does Zschopau not appear in the history of Bering Chemicals? I want to find out."

"Because he made no footprints that are worth remembering."

"I'd like some kind of confirmation on that statement, if you don't mind."

"I'll have someone look into it," said Hitomi.

Whenever she said that, Carl got suspicious, because she wasn't saying *I'll look into it*. What was wrong with looking into it herself?

"Someone. Would that be an intern, Hitomi?"

"Yes, an intern. Interns are eager, Carl."

Carl gulped the rest of the coffee. He swallowed and said: "Nów I can deal with your list. Fire away, Sakamoto. Hit me with your efficiency."

Six

Why can't I just take Hitomi's word for it? Carl wondered.

He was sitting in the heart of the city, where the river used to be. There was not a trace left of it. Only a white zone between the skyscrapers. From where the buildings and roads ended, the field of snow stretched underneath the trees of the parks on the riverbank, then bowed down to the flat strip that was once a river.

Now it was a white no man's land. The wind swept across the open space, hurrying from between the skyscrapers, whistling and whirling, blowing up snow from the ground. For the first time in twenty-four hours no snow was falling, but the thick gray clouds were amassing the next load.

"That looks like the motherload," said the man sitting next to the bizz jockey on the bench.

He wasn't shaking like the bizz jockey.

He wasn't rattling his teeth like the bizz jockey.

He wasn't incapable of lighting a cigar, like the bizz jockey.

And he didn't have trouble speaking without changing syllables because of freezing lips, like the bizz jockey.

I should just have left the whole thing to Sakamoto,

thought Carl. I'm insanely sitting by the river, only a couple of minutes from freezing.

The man next to him wore an old, floppy hat and a rumpled raincoat. How he managed not to get cold was a mystery, because he was obviously not wearing thick clothes underneath. He was tapping his right foot in the snow continuously. Under a battered nose and a scarred upper lip with a partial mustache he held a cigar in his mouth. He puffed and chewed. His shoulders were either moist from melting snow, or touched by dandruff, that was hard to tell.

Even though he had the appearance of a nervous wreck, a man on the run, nothing he said suggested any anxiety.

Of course not. After all, the man was Mach One.

He pointed at the clouds. "Don't you think? Wanna bet?"

Carl sighed, although the clattering of his teeth created a sound that resembled anything but a sigh. "Sure Mach-ck-ck," he said. "Let-t-t's talk business before I freez-zt-zt."

"You poor man," said Mach One. "You can hardly speak."

"Right-t-t. It's about-t-t B-B-Bering Ch-ch-chemicals." Then the bizz jockey cursed, or something like it. "T-t-this is ridiculous. Can't we go inside?"

"What about Bering Chemicals?" said Mach One.

"I need to know what happened to Ernst Zschopau."

Mach One looked away from Pappas, across the river, hiding the surprise on his face upon hearing that name.

Carl suddenly got revved up, his enthusiasm causing an abrupt end to the shaking and rattling. "The CEO of Bering denies even having heard of the man and I'm having a hard time believing him. Doctor Ernst Zschopau was very important back in those days, that much I remember. But all stories about him end decades ago. He was never fired. There are no reports about him quitting. He's just gone. I need you to find out why he left Bering."

While he spoke, Carl got up and started pacing through the snow, back and forth. When he was finished, he started shaking again.

"You think there could be something bad about Bering Chemicals?" he asked.

"I don't know," said Mach One. He had shaken himself loose from staring across the river. He puffed his cigar. "I can find out about Zschopau, I can do that. But it's a very thin thing. Why would a young CEO who's dealing with the problems of today be interested in the ancient history of his company? There are hardly any lessons to be learned."

"He looked at me funny," said Carl.

"He looked at you funny."

"You heard me, Mach," said Carl, suddenly irritated. "So now th-th-that's settled, I'm g-g-getting inside again. How can you stand this c-c-cold?"

"First of all," said Mach One, as he got up from the bench and started to walk back to the buildings of the city, with the bizz jockey beside him, "you are underdressed. If you are going to be outside, you need additional clothing. Especially on the feet and the head. They need to be warm."

"And second?" said Carl.

"I was in Siberia when I was young," said Mach One.

"In the capacity of Ross York? As a prisoner?"

"Perhaps. I was a prisoner in a Russian camp for a while, that's how one learns to stand the cold."

"You have been in t-t-the Gulag? I didn't know that."

"Officially I wasn't. Anyway, this cold here, it's nothing. It's warm enough to keep the wolves away."

For the first time since they met this morning, Carl laughed. The walking was good for him, the shaking faded.

"Were you a prisoner then?"

"Who knows," said Mach One, evasive as ever. "Did I ever tell you about our camp commander, the comrade in chief?"

"By all means."

"He was in constant pain because he had teeth problems. There was no dentist around and it was an urgent thing. So he checked the lists and it turns out there was a dentist among the prisoners."

"Surprise."

"Hardly. The Soviets had a knack for imprisoning useful people. Of course this dentist treated him. Removed a couple of molars. By way of revenge of course. Soon everybody in the camp knew he'd removed four molars too many, but by that time it was too late for the commanding comrade, of course."

"So the commander took revenge on him also?"

"Yes. Quite a bloody affair," said Mach One. He shook Carl's hand. "Thanks for the assignment. There's nothing like honest, hard work to make a man forget his past."

Carl stood there staring after the secretive man, as he walked off through the snow.

Seven

Truth be told, Mach One had no desire to forget any part of his past. He sort of toyed with his memories by telling anecdotes if it came in handy, telling them in a lighthearted way even if their true nature was tough and he could still feel the scars. Many memories had faded though, only to show their ugly heads after decades had passed, popping up unexpected and disappearing immediately after.

Picking up Doctor Ernst Zschopau across the East German border was one of these long gone memories. Of course he had only been a novice at the intelligence agency that exchanged Soviet spies and he had not been responsible, but the fiasco had paid off really bad for his superior. The shootout on East German soil had led to a political incident and someone had had to pay, but Mach One had been spared.

But it was not the fiasco itself that he was reminiscing as he drove across the rural landscape outside the city. Snow covered the fields, but the sky was clear today and the roads were dry.

No, it wasn't the fiasco, it was the scientist they had brought to freedom. He remembered Ernst Zschopau fairly well, because the Herr Doctor was a man entirely out of the ordinary. Of course there was the grandeur of his escape, the explosion and the colorful smoke that had put the Soviet agents in a fog and had allowed the Western agents to proceed with the task at hand. It had been a touch of magic, and he had continued that erratic behavior in the days that followed.

Mach One had been assigned, along with another colleague, to fly the scientist from the nearest airport out of West Germany immediately, and fly from one city to another to erase their tracks. During these couple of days he had gotten to know Zschopau as an unpredictable man who always had some sort of trick up his sleeve — a bit like a magician, indeed.

One particular night Mach would always remember. They were sitting in a hotel restaurant near the Vienna airport. The Doctor had to go and wash his hands, as he called it. Mach One, who was called Henri Washington at that time, and his colleague laughed about this, and by the time they were finished laughing the Doctor appeared at their table dressed as a waiter, a completely perfect disguise. Even his wild hair had been slicked back to fit the part.

"As you can see, gentlemen," said the Doctor, "I am perfectly capable of bringing myself to safety under many circumstances. You need not to fear for my safety."

They had been angry then, angry at the scientist's behavior. But now, all these years later, Mach One smiled.

I should have been impressed, not angry, he thought. Such a talented man!

He drove into the woods. He was closing in on his

destination.

Carl Pappas had just received a strong neck rub from his girlfriend when the phone rang. He picked it up reluctantly, because her touch and smell had intoxicated him. There was no medicine for the pains of work better than being thrown into the hands of this woman. He looked on, as her long legs beneath her underdress moved about the room, went to the bedroom, came back again and so forth. Right until he realized he was being connected, by a WCBN Radio receptionist, to William Nightingale, the Bering Chemicals CEO.

"Mr. Pappas, I do hope I'm not disturbing you at this hour."

"To be on the safe side I'll take that as a rhetorical question, William."

"Well, I'll be brief. I must apologize to you," said Nightingale.

"Apologize?"

"Yes. It was quite embarrassing. I must have had a blackout. Fancy being the boss of Bering and not knowing about Mr. Zschopau."

"Yeah, fancy that," said Carl, utterly confused. "You remember him nów?"

"Of course I do. It popped right back to me a couple of hours later. It woke me up straight in the middle of the night. But in retrospect it looked ridiculous and I hope I haven't embarrassed you."

"Why in the world would I be embarrassed?"

"Well, perhaps you felt my response made it look to the world like you had asked me a stupid question," said

Nightingale and he said it very monotonous, as if becoming bored all of a sudden.

"Yeah, whatever," said Carl. "So you feel better about it now?"

"I sure do. Thank you again for having me on the show. We're getting loads of positive feedback from our relations."

"Good. See you soon, William."

"If that man wanted to take away any suspicions of mine, he just failed miserably," Carl shouted across the room to wherever his girlfriend was.

Then he heard the shower. He looked at the clock on the wall. Plenty of time to check out the water quality.

As Pappas walked towards the bathroom he became agitated again. He didn't like liars.

Standing in the shadows at the edge of the forest, Mach One observed the industrial complex. Under the trees, there was no snow, so he could stand there comfortably. Also he could not be seen from afar.

The complex stood in the field, an uninhabited land behind a fence many dozens of kilometers in diameter. He had climbed the fence a couple of hundred meters behind him, in the middle of the forest.

The complex was hidden from the public's eye in many ways. Not only in a literal way, by being hidden in remote woods where no one was allowed to go. It was also hidden from public records. Mach One had had to do some deep probing through some pretty irregular channels to find this facility, linked not directly to Bering Chemicals, but only through some obscure firms in remote countries. Bering Inc.

was visible to the public and governmental scrutiny of modern times, but this facility was too remote from the official company to be on any accessible record.

And that's why Mach One had decided to take a look. Why would such a giant be hiding a complete factory? That would be interesting to know, even if it didn't bring any facts to the surface that would interest Carl Pappas. Knowledge is money, and that was the business of Mach One.

He just stood there for a whole hour, looking through binoculars he took from his forester's bag, checking out the premises. There were guards making their rounds of the buildings. A large black corporate limousine approached the main building across the main road, followed by another black car, albeit shorter. Stuff like that. It proved the factory was at least partially working. Other than that, nothing much seemed to be happening.

While he stood there, his thoughts drifted back to all those years ago, when he was working for Western intelligence agencies after he had done missions inside the Soviet Union for a long time — and been incarcerated too. For a while he had actually believed that the evil that had been done to him on the other side of the Iron Curtain, in the buildings of the KGB and all the way to the edges of Siberia, had to be countered by acts of good on this side. After a while he had come to see that, in the end, it was all the same. In the East they had for a long time believed that a socialist state was something worth fighting for, something worth suppressing people for. In the West they believed that democracy was worth fighting for, worth spreading around the globe. By now, Mach One believed both sides had been wrong all along. The last word was being spoken by money – always. The Communist block had come tumbling down because they went bankrupt. For a while, the West believed they had won. They didn't recognize their mutual enemy — money — until it hit them in a similar way.

He shook himself out of it. Dogs were appearing from the factory building's shadows and started running across the field. He realized they were barking; how the hell could he have missed them?

Eight

Mach raised his binoculars. The dogs were approaching the forest more or less in his direction. The distance was still hundreds of meters, but they would be here real soon.

It was time to go. He knew enough. Part one of his investigation had proven to be successful: an entire industrial complex, hidden from the world, owned by Bering Chemicals through a maze, unseen. Part two: finding Doctor Ernst Zschopau.

He had no idea which strategy to follow next.

He did know how to deal with the approaching dogs though. From his forester's bag he took a tiny bottle, opened it and turned it around. Stuff leaked from it, giving off an immediate unpleasant smell. He walked a couple of meters along the forest's border, emptying the bottle, and then withdrew between the trees.

Now Mach started running, while closing the bottle. His younger days were long gone and he was no longer interested in maintaining a good physical condition; actually, he couldn't care less. But on a day like this he regretted that attitude.

"If you do fieldwork," he panted, "you have to have a fieldworker's body."

While he ran towards the exact spot where he had climbed the fence, he suddenly heard how the barking of the dogs halted; the animals had obviously reached the small "odor curtain", consisting mainly of dog feces and urine. A nasty little cocktail, but it always did the trick.

He grabbed the rope he had left hanging there when he got in.

No need to rush any further. The guards would probably conclude that the dogs were on the trail of some forest badger or fox, pacing frantically along the line where Mach One had spilled the smell.

"Why do you have to spy on everybody all the time, Phil?" asked Carl.

He was sitting in the city's main library, a place close to the WCBN Radio building, but out of time because all the books were still there and there were no computer terminals anywhere to be found. This place was kept for people who wanted to read from paper, who wanted to be refrained from the constant distractions that computers offered. Surely, some of the stuff here was getting outdated, but it was a good place to think and do some deep research with serious focus.

Focus — you can't buy that online, Carl thought while he went through old folios full of ancient newspapers.

But there was nothing, nothing more than what he already knew: an important chemist criticized the East German government, as a result of which he was extradited during an exchange. He could not find anything about what had happened to Zschopau afterwards.

Until Phil Solo had barged in on him and asked him what he had been talking about with William Nightingale earlier that morning.

"Everybody knows you're here, Carl, but when I show up I'm spying. You have any idea how ridiculous that sounds?"

"Who knows I'm here? I didn't tell no one."

"How about Hitomi?"

"And how do you know I talked to Nightingale?"

"I got it from our receptionist by accident. Can we stop this infantile bickering, Carl? I feel like a kid when I'm with you. I worry about that sometimes, you bring out the worst in people," said Phil, he paced while he spoke, causing quite a stir in the quiet library.

"Oh that's alright," said Carl. "You piss off a lot of other people too, so I can live with that. It's a burden we all share at WCBN Radio."

Phil walked off.

Carl looked around him, trying to come to terms with that. Was he supposed to think that his boss was actually annoyed by something he had just said?

But before he could make up his mind, Phil was back with coffee in two paper cups.

"Thanks," said Carl. "I have use for that."

"Truth is, I don't care one bit who you talk to. I just thought it was interesting because you don't hold the chemical industry in very high regard. You're very critical of them. But that's not why I'm here. I suddenly thought, hey, what if you do an extra show, one every month, like a sort of *tour the time*."

"What the hell's a tour the time?" said Carl, a bit too loud for a place like this.

"You know, thoroughly going trough the history of a particular company or industry or event, seen from the bizz jockey's point of view. I thought of it when you mentioned this man, this Doctor Sch-Sch... what's his name. Would there be a great story to do?"

"I don't know, I'm not a fan of retrospectives. It's old wine."

"Your listeners love old wine. You pick your own topics, stuff that excites you. It'll be your vintage hour. Think about it. Once a month. Or wait, once every quarter, that could make it even more exclusive. You get a separate editorial team for it, some real diggers."

They were talking louder and louder. Now they were both laughing.

"One thing," said Phil. "Don't ask Sakamoto about her opinion yet. I don't want her to influence you."

"That's a laugh," yelled Carl. "It's yóu she'll influence!"

A young woman in a kind of uniform appeared.

"Excuse me, gentlemen," she said, looking almost angry, "that is absolutely not the way to behave in here. There's No Talking signs all over the place."

"But miss," said Phil, rising from his chair to face her eye to eye, "it felt like we were whispering. Honestly. You know, when you are with a man in a public place and you completely forget about yourself?"

The young woman gave Phil Solo a blank look and said: "I don't care what you do with a man in a public place, sir. As long as you're quiet."

It took the toughest coffee and the most remote place to drink it. Somewhere on a pier, looking out across the city harbor, Mach One sipped an Irish Coffee in order to get warm again. He sat close by the window, so he could look across The Great Lake, that was frozen over, basically a black hole with the light switched on. There was nothing to be seen and this suited him just fine.

Mach One worked entirely by instinct. He already knew enough about Bering Chemicals Inc. to know that if they wanted to hide something, they were probably very capable of it. Before delving into the purpose behind the hidden industrial complex, it was time to focus on Doctor Ernst Zschopau. Where Carl Pappas and Hitomi Sakamoto had to stick to official documents, press releases and the general media, Mach had other sources. But even these sources, reliable as they were, all had zero info on Zschopau for the last fifteen years. The man had quit Bering and then disappeared from the face of the earth. Gone he was from payrolls and phonebooks.

He sat there, looking into the white void, trying to find a way back in time and remember something crucial about the chemist. What would a man like Zschopau do once he had reached the free world?

Then it came back to him: Zschopau had been playful, showing some of the magic tricks. Behind the cheerful facade, the scientist had to have been a sentimental man.

And to Mach One, sentimental people had a predictable state of mind, which inevitably led to the same place.

Nine

The Zschopau family had fled the war-torn European continent a century ago. For many decades they had lived in the free world, away from armies and camps and ruined cities, in a comfortable house that had stayed in the family all these years. These had been fortunate times for a couple of generations, until Doctor Ernst Zschopau's parents decided they'd had enough of Western capitalism and emigrated to Eastern Europe to raise little Ernst as a proper socialist. First in the Soviet Union and many years later in the German Democratic Republic. In the process, they abandoned their family home in the free world.

It was to this house, Mach One had concluded, that the scientist was likely to return in the final years of his life. That is what men do when they're too old to live in the present, and too much alone: they return to their heritage. In the case of Doctor Zschopau this had to be the old family home and after some digging he found the house.

Mach One spent a lot of his time in his regular hotel no more than one city block from the WCBN Radio building. Close enough to look right into Carl Pappas' office on the seventeenth floor if he wanted; which he didn't. He walked from the lobby to the garage, took a rental car and drove out of the city. It took him just a few hours to drive to the city where the former Zschopau family home stood; he arrived there in the early evening, parked his car across the street and looked at it. A burlesque sign on the front read: *Theater of Magic*. Mach walked over in the icy early evening, mingling with the people who were entering the building, a large 19th century house of seven floors. It had a certain old-Germany quality to it, he thought.

The interior exceeded all expectations the name of the house might have raised. There was not one square meter left unattended; everything was covered with carpets and curtains, mysterious red lights, huge feathers and masks, there were sounds and smells, there was gypsy music. The ticket booth was manned by a woman wearing a Venetian mask. She might as well have been nude, for she was showing a lot of skin.

Slowly, an audience was building in the auditorium, located on the ground floor. The space had obviously been enlarged beyond the house's walls and must have taken up some of the neighboring buildings as well. There was no tribune, only small tables and chairs. Visitors could eat and drink at their tables during the show, or sit at the bar, which provided a very informal ambiance. To Mach One it looked like the proprietor was doing good business, for it was a weekday and the place looked like it was going to be a full house.

He took a table close to the stage and enjoyed a glass of red wine. Finally a voice sounded in the theater and the lights dimmed and a spotlight was directed at the center of the curtains: "Ladies an gentleman, thank you so much for showing up tonight. The maestro will be so pleased. Being the oldest magician still performing, every show is another victory for him and you have just made that possible one more time. Please welcome with a warm hand: The Great Mikado!"

The curtains swirled to the sides and revealed the magician himself, an old man in a black, lined costume with a long tail and red stitching, a tall black hat and a white beard. Entirely in contrast with all this were his glasses, that enlarged his eyes beyond all proportion, and the fact that he stood erect. He was ancient enough to be bend over like the first old man, but he had retained that straight spine in some miraculous way. He was of average height. He stood there motionless in the bright, warm light, taking in the applause.

Man must be a local hero, Mach One thought.

The applause took a couple of minutes, but The Great Mikado waited till the last handclap had disappeared somewhere between the curtains and the tapestries.

"Ladies and gentlemen," said the magician, "there are always new visitors among my loyal audience. Some have even come from far, I am told. So allow me to introduce myself: I am The Great Mikado and if you think that means anything, you are entirely right and entirely wrong at the same time, and figuring that mystery out is your personal quest."

Nodding heads created a wave through the audience. The magician then proceeded with some minor tricks. There was the card trick, the hat trick, the gloves trick, the magician's cape trick and the trick with the beautiful assistant.

For a while, Mach One resisted being charmed. He was only here looking for clues and at first regretted not sending someone else to do this job for him. In his life, entertainment was virtually absent for he simply never felt the need for it. But at some point he couldn't help smiling. It happened — and he should have seen this coming — when the dove came out from under the red napkin. The smile was to stay only a little while.

With a thundering boom, the dove and the magician and his assistant disappeared in a whirling cloud of pink smoke. An invisible orchestra struck up a violin-dominated overture.

Mach One felt excitement rush through him, a forgotten pleasure from his younger days. He smiled even more, thinking how the bizz jockey once again caused the unexpected to happen.

Then the smoke evaporated and a shock rushed over the rumpled private eye.

On the stage, a laboratory setting had appeared.

Finally, Mach One took off his overcoat and put it on his lap, on top of his hat. That didn't matter because the hat was floppy already anyway. But my, was it getting hot in there.

The stage reminded him of an old Frankenstein movie. At the end of the stage, in the back, a curtain had been risen to show a wall painted as a castle cellar. There was some green lightning on the remaining smoke on the stage floor. In the front stood a table with tubes and retorts, and some other small objects. Smoke billowed from the glasses.

The assistant had changed into a long, white laboratory

coat and a pair of rectangular glasses. She wide-eyed the audience and pouted her lips. It was probably a bit of well intentioned banter, but for Mach One it was out of place. For him, a serious moment had just begun.

The Great Mikado, still wearing his magician's clothes, picked up a plastic household box and held it high before the audience.

"This is made from polyethylene, as you undoubtedly know," said his assistant.

There was a slight tremor in the audience, some whispering.

"Of course this plastic is hardly degradable once it ends up as waste. But for The Great Mikado this is no trouble at all," she said, as she handed the plastic container to the magician. "Observe how he transforms the plastic into something entirely different."

The magician put the plastic household container in a small glass box that looked like an aquarium. Then he put a plastic tube into the aquarium, opened a tap and allowed a stream of fluid from a retort to pour into it.

By then, the music had stopped, so the hissing noise from the chemical reaction inside the aquarium was clearly audible for every member of the audience.

A thick, green fog emerged and clouded the stage. Only the legs and feet of the magician and his assistant, and the laboratory table could be seen.

Mach One held his breath. His thoughts were paused for the moment.

The smoke rose.

"Please show our wonderful guests the first results!" yelled the old magician. All this must have caused him considerable fatigue by now, but none was visible. He looked energized.

The assistant picked up the small aquarium and walked across the stage, stepped off the small stairs at the edge, and mingled among the audience, moving from table to table.

"It is perfectly safe to touch," said The Great Mikado.

Mach One also looked into the container. The white plastic household container had apparently melted, mixed with the fluid and then solidified into a transparent substance. It looked like water, but it was also solid. I also emanated substantial heat.

The woman walked back upon the stage.

"We will now take a sample from the magically converted polyethylene and demonstrate its new characteristic."

With her right hand, the assistant took a handful of whatever was in the aquarium — there were ooh's and aah's in the audience – and held it up for all to see. The white of the household container had converted into a gray, metallic color. What she held in her hand had no shape whatsoever, it was no more than a handful of clay.

While the audience stared, The Great Mikado had picked up a large painting from behind a curtain and held it up.

"Remember when you were young you used to attach a magazine centerfold to the wall with chewing gum or toothpaste," he said, evoking some timid laughter. "My new magical creation will do the same with this painting."

The painting indeed looked solid in its classic wooden frame. But with surprising agility for a man his age, The Great Mikado held it up, walked to a piece of wall what was at that very moment revealed by a curtain that swayed away magically, and a ray of light coming from nowhere. The assistant took two chewing gum sized pieces from the stuff in her hand, attached them to the back of the painting with a firm press of a thumb, and then assisted the magician as he slammed the painting against the wall with a firm movement.

Without a pause, they both stepped back, turned their faces to the audience and spread their arms.

Between them, the painting could be seen clearly. It hung on the wall. It hung there, as straight as could be, and the audience held its breath.

There was total silence in the theater for a full minute or so. Then Mach One couldn't take it anymore and started applauding like a maniac.

Everybody else joined in, exhilarated, as if they were all little children again for a few moments, breathing in the sheer power of illusion.

There was only one man in the audience who didn't feel that childhood excitement. That man was of course Mach One, who clapped his hands for a completely different reason: he had discovered Dr. Ernst Zschopau. For a few moments he was sitting on top of the world; even after all these years as a private investigator a small success was still a success.

There was no doubt in his mind.

Ten

The bizz jockey could not remember seeing his producer Hitomi Sakamoto so enthusiastic. Apparently she had left her stern and reserved personality behind at the door and now exposed something cheerful and youthful that he didn't know existed. It almost seemed as if she had forgotten all about their reason for attending the show in the *Theater of Magic*.

Mach One had refrained from contacting The Great Mikado, on Carl's specific instructions.

"I need him to talk out of his own free will. We don't want to scare him; he can always deny that he is Zschopau, and then we are nowhere. I will take care of that part myself."

"Myself," meaning him and Hitomi, because he needed her sharp mind to be present.

"Don't worry about it," Mach had said. "He's a cheerful old geezer. Remember: he likes a good prank."

So there they sat, watching a magician they didn't know, with no clue as to what to do next. While Hitomi simply enjoyed herself, Carl pondered about a possible strategy. Mach One had said the man liked a joke; that would be something to go with. But he was distracted more and more.

As the show progressed, Hitomi became enthusiastic and noisy. Truth be told, she was also drinking sake, which could have something to do with it. She grabbed Carl's arm and pinched it, and when he looked at her to say that it hurt, she smiled at him like a young girl.

Then she grabbed his hand to continue the pinching, and held it.

Carl could not withdraw his hand without using force, so he decided to let her, but all this movement was interfering with his train of thought.

I need something to break the ice before I can talk to the magician, he thought. Before the intermission.

But he could not move that train of thought forward, because the presence of Hitomi became all-encompassing as time went by.

"This is sooo great," she laughed out loud, during the next grand applause, as people got up from their chairs and there was general turmoil.

Even Carl stood up — he didn't want to be a spoilsport — and had Hitomi jump at him and threw her arms around his neck and hang there for a moment. The bizz jockey was taller than his producer.

A sweet aroma engulfed him, along with a warmth. The warmth of her body, yes, but also the warmth of this hidden side of Hitomi. Pappas had never had a problem with her rigorous personality, her matter of fact attitude, because it added to his own professionality on the job. There was no way you could do any lazy thinking with Hitomi Sakamoto in the room; and that was fine. But he also enjoyed seeing her this way.

Nevertheless he was relieved when the intermission started. He would just have to come up with an impromptu opening line in the coming minutes, as they walked backstage.

Above the old magician, in the *Theater of Magic*, the audience was enjoying the intermission, while his crew rearranged the stage and took care of all kinds of preparations for the second half of the show. That would be the shortest part of the evening, with only one major trick to be performed, but for now everybody was enjoying something to eat and drink, and some people were stretching their legs in the back yard, which had been transformed from an ordinary garden into a tiny fairytale's labyrinth.

But The Great Mikado simply sat in the basement, at his table with makeup mirror, in his dressing room. He took a sip from a small glass containing a limited amount of vodka, just enough to calm his nerves for the second half of the show; or for the benefit of nostalgia — he had never decided upon that. Along with the drink came a small dish of smoked and salted almonds.

No member of the crew ever disturbed him during the intermission, so the old magician was surprised to hear a knock on the door.

"Enter," he said.

In the mirror, a man and woman entered.

"Mr. Great Mikado?" said the man. "I'm Carl Pappas, the bizz jockey of WCBN Radio, and this is my producer Hitomi Sakamoto. Miss Sakamoto wants to be the next mikado world champion and she thought you could help her, but she's afraid to ask."

Hitomi, either completely taken by surprise or playing the part perfectly, took Carl's hand.

The old magician turned and smiled. Then he laughed. He could not remember having laughed so loud in years.

Eleven

"No. No. No," yelled Dr. Ernst Zschopau.

They were sitting in his dressing room. The old magician, being charmed by the bizz jockey's wit and the producer's smile, had quickly admitted to being Zschopau. He had abandoned that identity years ago and asked Carl and Hitomi to keep quiet about this.

But a few moments later, he was upset at something Carl had said.

"I have nót failed, Mr. Pappas."

The initial friendliness, initiated by Carl's impromptu banter, had suddenly vanished.

"I have nót amounted to zero. How can you say that? Listen, I appreciate your being honest, but you are merely talking about the career that is visible to the public. I have done things that are unseen, but they are important enough for you to swallow this insult, at least in the near future."

So far, the strategy of provoking the former East German scientist was not a promising one.

"You are upsetting me, when I need to relax for the rest of the show. You must leave now."

Carl and Hitomi stood up.

"Not you," said Zschopau to Hitomi. "We need to talk mikado, don't we?"

"Why, yes, please," said Hitomi.

She waved her hand behind her back, beckoning Carl to leave.

"I've never understood that mikado game anyway," said Carl as he walked out the door. "Where's the fun in that poking a pile of fallen bonsai trees? You'd have to be Japanese to get that."

He closed the door behind him, unsure as to whether everybody was merely playing a game and he was the only man with a serious mission.

He would have to trust Hitomi again.

Late that night, when both audience and crew had left the *Theater of Magic*, they sat in a living room on the top floor of the old house. Originally it had been an attic, but it had been redone with large windows in the roof and the walls, that gave it the impression of spaciousness. By now Zschopau had lit a cigar, poured vodka for the three of them, and started talking about his life. Obviously Hitomi had him thawed after Carl had been sent from the room during the intermission, earlier that night.

"I will prove to you that my life has not been in vain, you silly business disc jockey," Zschopau said. "I know how you are. Your whole life evolves around the economy and corporations and money. Do you think I became a magician just because I wanted to disguise myself? No. I am doing the thing I love most. Science was only a detour, albeit a long one.

I grew up with a notion of duty, and I have not been able to shake that off me until I was more than sixty years old. Too bad. So, I'm happy now, but while I was at it I have made scientific discoveries that are going to change this world forever."

"I apologize if I have offended you," said Carl. "I admit I know nothing about you, because you are shrouded by a thick fog. So please, tell me about what you have found. Because if you are going to change the world, you have to tell the world about it. I can offer you my audience. It's only ten million people, but hey, it's a start."

Zschopau laughed. "You are a funny man, Mr. Pappas. But things are not as easy as that. You see, my discovery, or invention rather, is in the hands of Bering Chemicals Inc. and I cannot get to it. And that, my dear visitors, is only the half of it. The good half, I might add."

"The good half? You left your invention at Bering Chemicals and they did nothing with it? What could be worse?"

"Something extremely destructive."

The doctor got up and started pacing the room. "That is, it has not yet been established. Bering Chemicals wanted to cover up the possible danger of my invention."

Carl said: "You let them do that? You ran away and gave up on your invention?"

Hitomi took Zschopau's sleeve and pulled him down softly, gesturing him to sit down.

"You have no idea, Miss Sakamoto, how a company like Bering can put pressure on a man to back off," the old magician said, and he looked around him with a sudden paleness.

"What's that cigar you're smoking, doctor?" asked Carl.

Both the doctor and Hitomi looked at him in a confused way.

"I'm sure it doesn't smell like..."

They all sniffed.

They sniffed again and turned heads.

Under the door, smoke was crawling into the room.

The open window, sucking the smoke right out of the room, prevented the trio in the attic of the *Theater of Magic* from being suffocated — but there was still the fire to deal with. They could hear it raging behind the door and even beneath them, the loud pangs as the flames ate through wooden beams.

Carl was hanging out the window looking down. The building was only burning on the floor below them. Once they got two floors down, they would be safe and be able to leave the building before the fire also started to spread downwards.

But Hitomi said: "We can't go through the door. I think if we open it, the fire will suck in all this fresh air and it will be all over us in a flash. We must climb down."

"I was hoping for a different tour of duty," shouted Carl. "Especially since there are no emergency stairs on the outside."

Twelve

Both Carl and Hitomi were quickly starting to lose their nerves. Flames were eating through the attic door, and reaching out of the floor beneath them like giant wings, graciously trying to lift the whole building off the earth.

"We can't go down here, even if there was a fire escape," said Carl. "Listen people, we need to come up with a solution real fast or we'll all be missing our next shows."

Hitomi's face was a grimace of fear, holding on to the window, looking down.

"Relax, my friends."

They turned and faced the doctor, only to be shocked by his calm and smiling face.

"You seem to be forgetting that you are in the company of The Great Mikado," he said softly. A sereneness seemed to have taken over the old magician.

He stepped between them, facing the window. "Stay with me," he said. Then he stepped on the windowsill, performing a delicate balancing act. He gestured them to join him.

So there they stood. Behind them the fire approached. Below them, the flames reached out to them with their scary yellow and red claws.

"What are you up to, Doctor?" yelled Carl. "Now would be a good time to share it with us. Because I am not going to jump, if that's what you think."

"Hold me tight," said Zschopau.

Carl and Hitomi each put one arm underneath the doctor's.

"Doctor!" shouted Carl. "Tell me!"

At that precise moment, as the flames behind them were close enough to feel, Zschopau threw his entire weight forward, dragging a surprised bizz jockey and his producer with him. As neither of them had a firm grip on the window post, they all fell face forward into the glow of the flames, and the darkness beyond that.

There wasn't even time to scream, as they plunged forward with the awesome pull of the gravity, six floors downwards, and the bizz jockey saw his life flash before him. The thousands of voices he had talked with came to him as if he was wearing expensive studio headphones, and then there was a powerful sound of something that resembled flapping of giant wings. Plastic materials hit his face and he let go of the doctor.

Then he plunged into some enormous air balloon that caught all three of them as it hit the ground, right before they would have.

They were launched into the labyrinth garden, spread out over the hedges and paths.

Carl looked up. Though the lights in the labyrinth had been turned off, he could see a giant inflatable whale lying in the garden. There was no mistake about it: it was a whale and it was huge for a toy, at least four meters long. Beyond it Hitomi rose from behind a low hedge. The inflatable toy whale, light as a feather, was pushed aside and there was Zschopau.

For a moment Carl considered asking about the source of the inflatable giant, but he let it go. "Nice trick, doctor. We'll do that again sometime. But we have to leave nów."

Zschopau smiled.

"The exit?" Carl growled between his teeth.

"Yes, OK, excuse me," said Zschopau, as he started hurrying through the labyrinth garden through the darkness.

"We have to get out and not draw any attention," the bizz jockey whispered. "I am sure for the moment it is better that we are presumed to have died in the fire."

It was a long and deep garden. By the time they reached the perimeter and the doctor started opening what must have been a gate, they were surrounded by complete darkness. In the distance, from behind the burning house, sirens were shrieking in the night, approaching.

Moving through the dark alleys behind the houses, Carl started his interrogation of the scientist. Hitomi closed ranks, looking back regularly to see if they were being followed, even though the alley was scarcely lit by old street lamps that had been turned down to the lowest possible level in order to save the city some money. They were practically invisible themselves.

"Tell me about your invention, doctor," Carl panted. "This is no time for secrets."

"You got that all wrong, Mr. Pappas. Secrets are my business. I'm a magician, remember?"

"You may be in trouble because of me," said Carl. "I talked

about you on the radio and had you located. Perhaps I have stirred something that was better left alone."

"Or perhaps you are just being paranoid."

They stopped at a dark intersection of alleys. For a moment they listened, then Zschopau hurried into another dark tunnel. Again he appeared much younger and physically fit than one would expect from such an old man.

"Many, many years ago, when I was employed by Bering, I built a new kind of synthetic that can be used for almost anything from toys to cars to pacemakers, or artificial body parts like a liver, that have one thing in common: they break down naturally after usage."

While Carl panted, he noticed how the breath of the old magician stayed regular all the time.

This old comrade is in better condition than I am, he thought.

"And when I say naturally, I mean one hundred percent natural. It leaves no trace."

"But that's... astonishing," said Carl. "So Nightingale was right."

"We're putting the Doctor on your show this week," said Hitomi from behind.

They crossed a silent road. Behind them were houses, but in front of them a dark city park loomed.

"We gettin' in there, old man?" said Carl. "Is that wise?"

"Trust me," said Zschopau.

He seemed to be speeding things up, much to Pappas' dismay.

"So why was this wonder synthetic never brought to the

market?" said Carl, trying to divert his attention from the utter darkness of the park and his own aching body. "And can we please slow down a bit?"

Suddenly Zschopau stopped. "I discovered a fault," he said. "The synthetic's initial breakdown will most likely be reversed after a hundred years or more, and then turn certain molecular combinations into a very toxic compound."

"What do you mean 'most likely'?" said Carl. "And how can you know what happens in a hundred years? No one can know that."

"Not for the full hundred percent," said Zschopau. "But I ran tests for a decade and I've come to the conclusion that this is the only reasonable outcome. Of course you won't know for sure after a hundred years or so, but still. I've not created a synthetic that would change the world, but destroy it. Very sad."

"Come now, don't be sad!" a loud voice sounded from nearby.

From out of the darkness of the park, men emerged.

"This is not good," Hitomi whispered.

You didn't need a sharp mind like Hitomi Sakamoto's to notice that the men who came from the dark had uncivilized intentions.

"Don't be sad, because we are going to relieve you from everything that troubles you. You'll feel much better in a moment," a large, muscular young man said.

It was very dark, so they would never be able to identify these men afterwards.

Suddenly a couple of men lurked forward and grabbed them. Carl was hit in the face, and held by his arms, unable to do anything about everything. But Hitomi kicked her first attacker in the crotch and struck the second one in his throat, sort of pushing his Adam's apple like a button. All the way in.

They also never had a chance with Dr. Ernst Zschopau. He acted with true *Jekyll and Hyde* bravado, pushing back his magicians cape, making a couple of swift movements and bringing out a light so bright, it blinded everybody. Perhaps it was a rescue flair from a ship, who knows. But while it did its work, he moved his other arm under his cape and then the whole situation escalated.

Exploding fireworks seemed to emanate from The Great Mikado's body itself. Sky rockets whooshed away in all directions. He threw the flare away towards the attacking men and then held up a Catherine wheel, a whirling circle of fire, moving it around. Then, to make his point, he started throwing firecrackers around, not the light ones that kids can use on New Year's Eve, but the heavy stuff. The chaos was total.

Within one minute, they were alone again.

"Follow me," said Zschopau. "They won't fall for that a second time."

His cape flapped in the night as he sped up into the darkness of the park. Pappas and Sakamoto followed.

"I can't believe this," Carl muttered. "If the action keeps building at this speed, we'll be in a global war before midnight!"

The night closed in behind them. There was no way they were going to be seen from anywhere.

Thirteen

They were driving in the night. The highway was clean and dry and the sky had momentarily cleared. That was good, because snowfall was the last thing they needed right now, they wanted to get as many miles between them and the *Theater of Magic* as possible.

"We'll find out what's going on later," Carl had said as he had walked into the rental firm's office, a small business with night service.

Hitomi sat behind the wheel of the rental car. Carl sat next to her, turned to the back to face The Great Mikado. The old magician had taken off his cape and put it behind his head, with the intention to take a nap. But he was awake nonetheless.

"I was fired by the corporation," said Zschopau. "Basically they've decided to wait till I die. Then they can bring the synthetic to the markets and get rich."

"That's ridiculous," said Carl. "And then after a hundred years, when your chemicals starts to re..."

"Regroup."

"Regroup, yeah. Then they're in the shithouse, because

everybody will know what they did."

"They will be dead and buried long before that problem occurs," said Hitomi. "Don't you see? They'll just be incredibly rich and famous and live out their lives in luxury."

"Precisely," said Zschopau. "If anything goes wrong, it will affect their grandchildren maybe, but not them."

"Stop this car," snarled Carl to Hitomi, pointing to a parking sign on the side of the highway. "Go on, get off this road, I can't believe this shit!"

He appeared to be sniffing and puffing through his nose, lifting his arms in the air. As soon as Hitomi had stopped the car at a parking lot, he got out, slammed the door shut and paced around, cursing.

After a few moments, he got back in, obviously very angry. "Why haven't you gone to the press, doctor? I can't believe you can live with yourself."

"Will you calm down please?" said Hitomi. "There will be a perfectly reasonable explanation I'm sure. Isn't there, Ernst?"

Now it was time for Zschopau to be annoyed. "Of course there is. I spent decades developing a failure. I will look like a fool."

"Who cares?" Carl's response resembled a dog biting.

"Anyway, who in the world is going to believe a scientist who failed to begin with? All I have are theories. Besides..."

The old man looked out the window, at the passing cars.

"Besides what, Ernst?" Hitomi asked softly.

"All my notes and formulas and test results are in possession of Bering Chemicals anyway. I cannot get to them. I dare not risk a legal procedure, they have too many lawyers."

Hitomi started the car again and drove off, back to the

highway.

"Besides, I don't care anymore. It is almost twenty years ago now, I am old, I am enjoying a few years as a magician, doing the thing I've always wanted. It took me fifteen years to build the *Theater of Magic* and its show. I have long grown tired of the wheelings and dealings of the science community."

"Have they threatened you, Dr. Zschopau?" Carl asked.

"Yes. But that was a long time ago. I suppose they've lost track of me. I hope."

"This stinks, I can't believe stuff like this still goes on," said Carl. "And shame on you for abandoning your invention. I can assure you that I will not leave this thing alone."

"They've probably bribed the government," said Zschopau. "The whole factory complex where I worked is surrounded by a sort of no man's land, where no authority ever shows up to check up on things."

"You're saying they're actually *manufacturing* that creepy synthetic of yours right now?" Carl said sarcastically.

"I don't know the status right now," said Zschopau, still looking out the window. His voice started to fade a little, as if he had enough of the whole topic. "Years ago I did some hacking and sniffing, but I soon gave up. I was afraid they'd find me again. I wanted to stay clear of these people, as you can see."

"Well, yes, I sympathize," said Carl.

"All I know is that they're still operative, although not under the Bering flag. They may have been piling up my compound all these years, getting it ready."

"Pedal to the metal, Sakamoto," said Carl. "We need to get

the professor his papers." He turned to the back of the car again. "If you get your papers, you can prove your point, old man?"

"Not necessarily," said the doctor weakly.

"That's encouraging. Well, at least you can get other scientists to evaluate your research. That's worth something, isn't it?"

There was no answer. Dr. Ernst Zschopau had fallen asleep.

Fourteen

Phil Solo, the managing director of WCBN Radio, noticed something strange. During every break of The Boardroom, the bizz jockey and his producer were frantically discussing something. It was starting to annoy him. What was so important that they had to confer almost all the time, making sure no one could hear them? And more than that: how come there was something important going on without his knowledge?

He couldn't stand that, although he had learned to trust Pappas and Sakamoto through the years. The only person he didn't trust was the bizz jockey's sound engineer; that man could switch on a microphone right under your nose and listen in his sleep. How could you be sure Don Wozniak wasn't listening in on you? The answer was: you couldn't. He didn't like that and he didn't like this.

"We're grateful for another night of wisdom from the world's number one bizz jockey," the pre-recorded voice of the WCBN Radio announcer said through the speakers. "This concludes tonight's episode of The Boardroom. On behalf of Carl Pappas I say that WCBN Radio hopes you will be listening in at the same hour tomorrow. And now, after the break, you will be updated on the price of fame. What are the current price tags of today's celebrities? Who are the newcomers, and who fell behind? Forget the old movie stars and pop heroes. The most famous people today are the heirs to the great family brands of the world. So be informed. Stay tuned."

Phil walked towards Carl and Hitomi, who were standing in the studio as the guests were escorted out by another member of the Boardroom team.

"What are you guys up to?" said Solo, clearly interrupting another heated argument. "I can tell you I get very nervous when you folks are chatting away like this. Capiche?" He spread his arms, palms up, grinning like an Italian photo model, in his Armani armor. "Maybe I can help?"

"Not now, Phil."

"Sure. Call me when the shit hits the fan, is that it? Oh Phil, please bail me out?"

"Yeah, something like that," said Carl. "Listen, you can't control things when they're not ready to be controlled. This is just a rough diamond we're trying to polish here. You'll be updated when... if... uh. Listen, that item after The Boardroom, is that really necessary every month? I don't like it. All that gossip."

"Don't worry," said Phil, as he walked briskly out of the studio room. "They won't be talking about you."

"Is he angry again? How do I do that?" said Carl.

"Carl Evangelos Pappas, stay focused," said Hitomi. "You are suggesting we break into a factory. I don't get paid to do stuff like that."

"Break in, break in, that's not the right term, Hitomi. Zschopau invented that stuff, he just wants to look at his papers one more time before he dies. Any judge will buy that."

"He is not dying, Carl. It's called burglary."

"Ma... My man says it can be done."

"Your man?"

"Says it's a walk in the park."

"You want to break into a factory and you want an eighty-year-old to show you the way," said Hitomi.

"There is no other way. He'll remember where his papers are once he's on the spot."

"I don't like this, Pappas. I don't like this at all. Why would his papers be still there? I'd put lawyers on it."

"Because if you get an official warrant, they'll simply deny having any papers after all these years. Oh come on, you're just chicken, Sakamoto. It's a remote factory, it's empty, there's only a few men with, well, dogs, and I have a trick for them. Trust me, I know how to do this."

"Thanks to your man."

"Yes. And I think these papers will still be on the premises, because it's a safe place."

"You are saying," whispered Hitomi with her most serious tone, her small dark eyes piercing the bizz jockey's, "that your so-called friend has the ins and outs on how to smuggle Ernst in there, get the papers, and walk out again without a smudge on my legal record?"

"You've had a few brushes with authorities on behalf of The Boardroom before, Hitomi, don't go all wooshy on me now. And yes, that's what I'm saying. You trust me or not? Listen, I'm not looking forward to this either, but Zschopau's story is just too outrageous. We have to make a move."

The producer sighed. She was obviously going through an internal struggle. Then Don Wozniak entered the room, feeling like a big shot. He came next to Hitomi, put his arm around her and said, with a pizza breath: "Hitomi, the worldwide economic top brass is once again impressed by this impeccably produced show."

Immediately she released the arm, threw it off, and walked away. These men — it was just too much right now. One was nuts and the other... a sound engineer.

===

In one of his temporary homes, a hotel nearby the WCBN Radio building, overlooking the frozen river, Mach One was on the phone with one of his many aides and informants. He didn't like what he was hearing. Already it was clear that the fire in the *Theater of Magic* had been the work of an arsonist. And a professional one at that, because the fire had been lit on the floor below the attic, in all four corners, to make sure it created an impenetrable zone that sealed off all escape routes. According to his source, the police were entirely in the dark about how the occupants got out. They would soon trace the bizz jockey and Hitomi Sakamoto and Dr. Zschopau down and start asking them questions. The theater crew members who had been the last to leave the building must have known that The Great Mikado himself was still on the top floor. There would be a lot of explaining to do real soon.

But the police could be convinced. It was the arsonist that worried Mach. He disconnected his cell phone and stared.

One thing he had not been able to figure out. Should he reveal himself to both Carl Pappas and Dr. Zschopau as the former Henri Washington, secret agent to one of the Western powers, who helped the doctor to cross the Iron Curtain? And to what purpose? To drink vodka with Zschopau and discuss old times, perhaps even laugh at the silliness of it all? And then? Talk about his other identities of the past? So far, Pappas knew only the name "Ross York", and Mach One liked it that way. To reveal his connection to "Henri Washington" would be to expose himself further.

Without exception, he had regretted every unnecessary exposure he had ever allowed in his life.

How unfortunate, he thought. The doctor would be a fine man to drink vodka with. He would understand a lot.

But not now. Maybe later, when this was all over and the bizz jockey had turned his back on Zschopau once more. Maybe then. It would be nice though. Even bad memories from his adventures in the former USSR had, by now, been reduced to dinner and after dinner stories.

And to return to the tasks at hand: it was clear to him that the bizz jockey might be in some kind of danger. Obviously the arsonist had been sent by a source from deep within Bering; he didn't have to check that out. They would have covered their tracks. No, it was the bizz jockey himself that needed to be watched. The man had asked Mach One a thousand questions about the remote factory. It was obvious to him that the notorious Carl Pappas was putting on his radio detective coat again. Mach decided to keep his eyes and ears open, and locked on target. Locked on the bizz jockey.

Because usually it worked like this: if the arsonist fails, the place will be swarming with gunmen real soon.

Fifteen

Luck had nothing to do with it. The dogs simply had to be indoors because of the weather. No one in his right mind would walk around voluntarily in this cold, especially now that it had started to snow again. Bringing dogs along with you would have been an act of animal cruelty, punishable by law.

The factory complex lay unidentifiable in the landscape, a silhouette in a black and white photograph. On the edge of the terrain, far left, were two spheres; twin giants towering over everything else. They were higher than a space rocket launch tower from Cape Canaveral. Their round forms demanded attention in the landscape, especially next to the rectangular forms of the other buildings. Each one smaller than the spheres, they stood huddled together: an old factory with a chimney, a couple of supplemental smaller constructions and an office building, surrounded by all kinds of smaller stuff, barracks and sheds and probably a guardhouse, and even an old-fashioned phone booth.

Thanks to his secret source, Carl Pappas had been able to steer his party through the fence in the forest. That part had been easy. But going through these woods on gut feel proved to be difficult. It was dark between the trees, old pines that had littered their living room with millions of branches. While they stumbled and fell and tried to find their way to the no man's land where the factory stood, they noticed it had started to snow. Not many snowflakes made it this far, through the thick canopy of pine needles, but some did. The forest stood cold and indifferent to human suffering. At some point, the howling of a wolf could be heard in the far distance... or was it?

It took them a full hour to cross the woods. But when they finally arrived at the edge, the thickening snow came like a comrade in arms. Hitomi had proposed that they all wore white overalls, so they were now entirely invisible in the landscape. Even if they made a sound, it would not carry very far in this weather.

Strangely enough there was no fence in the immediate vicinity of the buildings. There were street lamps all over the complex, but they hadn't been switched on. The snow limited visibility, but it was still early in the afternoon.

And so they crossed the terrain without any difficulty. While they did that, the weather upped the ante. Within a couple of hundred meters, the weather progressed from merely falling flakes to an arctic wind, propelling tiny blades in their faces. The buildings in front of them disappeared from sight.

Moments before they had to turn back — if there was such a thing, because the forest behind them had disappeared as well — they reached the outer buildings.

"Just in a nick of time," shouted Carl.

Hitomi reprimanded him for making a noise by kicking him, with painful results.

They followed the doctor as he walked past the first building, nothing more than a barrack. When they reached the other side of it, they were finally out of reach of the snow. A large building with an extended roof hovered over them. The grip of the wind had faded here.

Dr. Ernst Zschopau pointed the thumb of his mitten towards the barrack. Hitomi tried the handle, but it was locked. She made a "now what?" gesture with her hands.

But the doctor smiled. He removed both of his mittens, clamped them under one arm, put one hand into his parka and brought out a key.

Pappas and Hitomi stood there dumbfounded as the old magician put the ancient key in the lock and opened the barrack without any delays. Then he walked in and beckoned them to follow him.

As they closed the door, the snowstorm outside, feeling completely ignored, decided to turn to more drastic measures and started taking on the form of an outright blizzard.

===

Through the raging blizzard, a black limousine moved. Slowly it entered the parking lot by the office building, made a few turns and stopped by the entrance.

The chauffeur got out, ran around the car and opened one of the passenger doors. William Nightingale got out holding on to his scarf and his small suitcase, and quickly disappeared into the office building.

He was greeted by a uniformed guard and two dogs.

The dogs were unimpressed. They quietly sat on both sides of the man's boots.

"Welcome Mr. Nightingale," said the guard. "It seems you got here just in time."

"Blasted storm," said Nightingale as he walked straight past the man into the reception area. He dumped his suitcase and his scarf on one of the benches and turned to face the guard and the chauffeur.

"Please give me a security update," he said in a demanding tone.

"Everything is normal, sir," said the guard. "The security system is operational in both the main factory building and the laboratory. Green lights all over."

"I don't share your optimism. In this weather, anyone can simply walk over without being seen."

"Anyone who walks this blizzard, loses all sense of direction within meters, sir. There is no way someone can walk onto the lot now."

"You are not listening. We are facing serious opposition right now and it is vital that this place remains absolutely safe. What if someone already walked here before it started snowing?"

The guard was starting to lose his nerve. "Well, I..."

"When was the last round with the dogs?"

"One hour ago, sir."

"Do it again."

"Impossible, sir, this blizzard is too dangerous for them, and they'd also be unable to smell even a pig's farm."

With a swift movement, the Bering Chemicals CEO moved forward and stood very close to the guard. They were face to face.

"A pig's farm, you say?"

"I... It was just a matter of speaking, sir."

"Do the round. With or without the dogs. I'll wait here. Fifteen minutes from now if you're not back I will call the administration and tell them you're fired. Get that? Where's your buddy?"

"He's in the guardhouse, sir," said the guard as he rushed through the exit.

The dogs stayed put.

Nightingale took out his cell phone.

"Hi. No. They're doing a round now. Any news about that bizz jockey yet? OK. If things get worse, we may have to move things out of here. Start preparing a full scale evacuation right now."

===

The barrack was old and dusty. Waving their pocket lights around, they could see that immediately. No one had been in here for a very long time. Pappas, Sakamoto and Zschopau stood in a portal, amongst old furniture like a table, chairs and an old fashioned clergyman's desk. There was an internal window with an office behind it. Plus a corridor that led further into the darkness of the barrack.

"You've kept this key for twenty years?" asked Carl, still astonished.

"There are many keys in this world," said Zschopau. "This

barrack was built to bring certain materials directly into the underground laboratory without having to go through the main building. There's one chamber along the corridor that has a stairway leading down. Since it looks nothing has changed here, chances are we can walk right down."

"I find that hard to believe," said Pappas.

But before he could explain why, they heard something in the dark corridor in front of them. Hitomi grabbed the bizz jockey's arm and held on tight. Something or someone was approaching them.

Sixteen

The industrial complex of Drenz was located in a remote rural area, completely out of view. It was surrounded by an immense forest on all sides, through which only one single road led to the entrance. Long ago, in a time when industry moguls could pretty much do as they pleased, it had been built here. Its architects had also taken care of a couple of wide gaps in the forest by planting thousands of pine trees. What had looked a bit silly at first, all these rows of baby pine trees in a sandy field had, after many decades, filled up the gaps seamlessly. Fifty kilometers in one direction stood the first farm, the other directions were uninhabitable mountains and swamps and forests.

Drenz had long functioned as a place to secretly work on a plethora of machines and weapons, but had remained mostly dormant for the past decades. It was owned by a shell company on the Cayman Islands, in order to hide the real owners, Bering Chemicals Inc. The ancient ties with the government had long been forgotten, except for a few officials who were bribed to make sure no questions were asked and no flight paths were ever scheduled over this area.

Yet Drenz was not entirely dormant. A couple of times a year, scientists from Bering would arrive by helicopter or limousine, talk to the guards a bit, and then enter the factory building for one or two days, and then leave again. In their absence, the guards were not allowed to go in. Basically all they did was watch the computer screens with the alarm status of the factory and the underground laboratory, and walk rounds on the complex every few hours until they were replaced after their tour of duty.

So the Drenz complex was maintained carefully, because it was yet to have its finest hour...

But today, Bul Dallas, senior guard on the Drenz terrain, did not feel as if he was taking part in something grand. He felt belittled by this man, this Nightingale, whom he didn't even really consider his boss. Dallas was on the payroll of a security firm. He'd never seen Nightingale before in his life, but his own boss had called him earlier that day to instruct him to be extremely polite to the CEO who was one of the real owners of Drenz, and also their client. From the way Nightingale had behaved the minute he arrived, Dallas had concluded it was best to be subservient and ask no further questions.

But none of that meant he had to like it and so he didn't. And getting around without the dogs spooked him; the snow stung in his face and hands like shards of glass, and he realized he wasn't dressed properly. Bul Dallas was a large man, a former forklift chauffeur who had sometimes gotten out of his forklift to lift crates himself if the equipment didn't do it the way he liked it. His whiskers had travelled with him from another time, large and dark, and were now catching snowflakes and turning white immediately.

===

Three pocket lights flashed simultaneously. Two yellow eyes lit up, and then the bulk of a large, furry animal turned and sped back into the darkness of the corridor.

"Take it easy, people," said Carl, though his voice was shaky. "What was that anyway? A fox?"

"Smaller," said Zschopau. "Here's the room."

It was unlocked. Beyond a few tables and empty cupboards, in the back of the room, they found a stairway leading straight into the ground. In the pitch black, Carl went down first, lighting the steps with his pocket light. After a long climb they arrived on a level a couple of meters below the ground, a tunnel leading in one direction only. It was damp and cold. There was a mild smell of fungus. The tunnel was made entirely of concrete, and echoed incessantly.

They hurried through the tunnel.

"How come this place has no alarm system?" said Hitomi.

"It does," said Zschopau, "but I wouldn't worry about it. I know what I'm doing."

"That's funny," Carl panted. "I came up with this stupid plan, and I have no clue."

The tunnel ended. There was a solid, albeit rusty metal door. In the center was a wheel.

"Don't tell me all we have to do is turn the wheel and we get in," said Carl. "That would be a laugh."

The old magician grabbed the wheel, but he couldn't turn it. "You try it, Mr. Muscles," he said, smiling to Carl.

"I used to say I'm too old for this shit," said Carl, as he started turning the wheel, yanking at it with all the force he could muster. "But in your presence... I'm... a... young... man!"

The door swirled open towards them. Whatever was inside, it was warm and dry.

Zschopau raised a hand, gesturing them to wait. "This tunnel brings us straight into a utility room, where the central heater is and the electricity is distributed. Beyond that is a corridor, and the first room is where my papers were kept in a vault. The alarm system was built in to guard only the inside of the factory above us and the important parts of the underground laboratory. Not the utility room, if I remember correctly. The only alarm console for this entire floor is located in the front, where the elevator is."

"How fast can we move in, get your papers from the vault, and be out again?" asked Carl.

"That would depend on whether they've changed the combination to that vault," chuckled the doctor.

He ducked and stepped in through the small iron door. Carl and Hitomi followed him, their hearts throbbing in their throats.

The utility room was softly lit. They could hear the rushing of water through central heating pipes, and the humming of a pump.

The doctor stood still by a table, took out a pen and a piece of paper, and started drawing a map of the laboratory.

"We're here," he said. "That there is were I used to keep my papers."

"I don't know," said Carl. "Do we take it for granted that

they've not moved your papers in twenty years?"

"Carl Evangelos Pappas," snapped Hitomi, with a whispering voice, "we have nothing else to go on. Stop mentioning the obvious and get on with it."

Seventeen

Bul Dallas entered the guardhouse. His colleague Jock Belarus was staring intensely at the console with the green alarm lights, and a couple of monitors revealing the closed surveillance circuit. Their weak black and white imagery was motionless. It was not a modern security system, but it could detect a mouse if one ever dared enter the laboratory or the factory.

"Boss is here," said Bul.

"I know," said Jock, a tiny man compared to Bul, with a boney nose sticking out of his pale smoker's face, short thin hair combed to stand up resulting in a chaotic mess. The security firm didn't have uniforms in his size, so he was swimming in it.

None of this mattered, because Jock Belarus didn't care and he was very good at his work.

"I'm on the console," he said, toneless and loud, as if performing on stage. "It's too cold even for alien life forms. Relax."

"I can't relax," snapped Bul. "I'm supposed to make a complete round and then report back to that guy, or else I'll be fired on the spot. I can't believe he said that. I'm thinking about resigning before he gets to me. You know, keep the honor to myself."

"You are going to do nothing of the sort," riposted Jock. "What will your Betty say? That man can't fire you, he's not your boss."

"He can put the thumbscrews on our employer, that's what he can do."

"Rubbish. They'll simply relocate you. Listen, he's just trying to intimidate you."

"Yeah, well, I couldn't see a tit if I was sucking one. The snow's like a wall. I almost lost my way. Even if someone was breaking in right now, we wouldn't be able to get there."

"Go to the man and tell him everything's fine. What's he going to do, check your footsteps?"

They both laughed.

Jock got up and poured his buddy a paper cup of coffee. "Here, have this," he said as he handed over the cup. "And then you go."

Bul took a sip. Then his eyes bulged and he spit the coffee right in Jock's face.

===

Three concrete steps led them up from the utility room onto the level where the laboratory was. The corridor in front of them was bathing in a soft light, and the temperature was even higher here. Almost every room along this corridor was visible through glass.

They now rushed, following The Great Mikado into the first

room on their left. It was unlocked. The scientist moved in, hit a light switch and entered.

"I'm not sure if turning lights on is a good idea," muttered Carl, but no one paid attention.

The room was obviously an archive; there were racks of shelves, floor to ceiling and wall to wall. The scientist ran between the racks, turned a corner, hesitated, turned another corner, and finally stopped in front of a large metal closet.

"That's the vault?" asked Carl.

"Yes. It may look like a cupboard, but it's really a vault."

"It doesn't look dusty, so they've been here," said Hitomi. "Let's hope your papers are still there."

"And my diskettes," Zschopau said with an air of nostalgia. "Those magical floppy disks." He started turning the wheel of the vault, his ear pressed to the metal door.

"How can he hear anything at his age?" the bizz jockey whispered to Hitomi.

The vault door swung open. The bizz jockey and his producer looked on with their mouths open.

"They didn't change the combination?" Hitomi said, before her boss could.

Zschopau just smiled at them, turned and started taking things out of the vault. There was a valise old enough to belong to Carl Pappas' grandfather, ancient leather entirely worn out. It was stacked to the brim. There was also a box full of floppy disks.

"It's all here," said Zschopau, as he gave Carl the diskettes box and kept the valise himself.

"We could do a live show from this place," whispered Hitomi. "Wouldn't that be cool?"

===

"What the..." screamed Jock, his face dripping with coffee.

"Red light!" yelled Bul, pointing at the console.

There it was: a red light blinking.

Jock swiped his sleeve across his face and turned to the alarm system panel. "That's the laboratory," he said. "Damn. Go, go, go!" He jumped up.

They ran for the door, but as soon as it opened, they hesitated.

"Lord have mercy," said Jock.

"That's what I said. Get mittens and safety glasses. We can't get to the factory building unprotected in this blizzard."

Jock opened a locker that stood close to the door and started rumbling through the inside. "Get the dogs?"

"I'm not taking the dogs in this weather, we're responsible. Got your gun? We'll go by the office building and see if Mr. Nightingale and his chauffeur can join us. Hurry!"

While putting on the mittens and safety glasses, they disappeared behind a curtain of snow.

Eighteen

The cooling installation, cylinder shaped, towered under the factory roof. Dr. Ernst Zschopau stood before it and spread his arms, the valise bungling from one hand, the installation vaguely lit by their flashlight.

"It's all in there, my dear friends. Allow me to introduce to you: Z-mere, the plastic that loves nature and will be loved in return."

"You sound like an advertisement," Carl Pappas said, looking up. "And what are these?"

Behind the cooling installation was a wall of black barrels.

"That's a more finished version of Z-mere," said Zschopau. "The cylinder contains the product in an incubative state."

"Good. Now that we've seen it, we have to go," said Hitomi. She took both men by the sleeve and jerked them away. "This is crazy, we have to go down again, come on."

As they ran back, towards the elevator and the stairway that led down to the laboratory, Carl asked: "Why are they keeping your, eh, Z-mere in that cooler? Have they been keeping it there all these years?"

"I don't know. Maybe they made some new batches, maybe

they've stored more in the cooling spheres outside, who knows? But it looks magnificent, don't you think?"

"You turned your back on science, Ernst. Remember?" said Hitomi, who was now behind the scientist, pushing him with all her might. "Hurry!"

Then all the lights in the factory were switched on. First there was the flickering of the luminescent tubes, hundreds of them, and then there was full, blinding light all over the place.

"Halt!" a man shouted. "Stand still or we shoot."

Immediately they took a turn, disappearing behind the cooling silo. Behind them, shots were fired.

"No, you can't shoot in here, idiot," a second voice shouted.

The professor slammed the valise against Carl Pappas' chest. "Hold that for a moment," he said. Then he ran into an alley towards an outside wall. Suddenly he stopped. There was a flash and a roaring sound, and something that resembled a rocket swooshed through the air, away from the scientist, up in the air and straight into one of the huge windows at a height of approximately five meters. There was shattering of glass, and then the blizzard entered the building like a troupe of elephants. Within moments, the wind had created a draft between the broken window and the outside door that had just been opened, and it felt like all the snow in the world now wanted to pass.

Bul and Jock had come in through a small personnel door at the bottom of a huge hangar door. The woodwork was no longer strong enough to resist the gale. Planks started to splinter and were blown away.

The two guards looked around them, overcome by all that sudden action. They didn't know what was more worrisome: the wind shaking up the building from the inside, or the cooling silo being accidentally hit by a bullet, now moaning like a dying wolf...

The old magician ran back to his friends, and together they got out of the blizzard's way and ran down the stairs into the laboratory below. Behind them there were loud noises, rumblings in the hysterical hiss of the blizzard. By the time they got down, sirens started to wail above them.

"That must be the cooling system," Zschopau panted as the ran through the empty laboratory corridor. "Too bad!"

"Will it... explode?" Carl said as they jumped off the three steps into the utility room.

"Not necessarily," said the professor. "It's a newer system I'm not necessarily familiar with, but if it breaks down, the Z-mere would normally warm up and solidify, and become useless — but with these temperatures... who knows!"

Carl stopped at the other end of the machine room. "Where's... the tunnel? It's gone!"

"It's just accidentally hidden. Follow me," said Zschopau, as he stepped through a narrow space between two boilers and disappeared.

When Carl was finally running through the tunnel, he noticed Hitomi had fallen behind. "Hitomi, what are you doing?" he yelled.

She was pushing the outer door to a close. "What does it look like, Pappas," she yelled back.

Before they reached the stairway into the barrack, she

added: "Are you through with asking redundant questions?" But the nervous smile on her face softened the message considerably.

===

William Nightingale was trying to move through the snow that was blown into his face like a solid wall. His chauffeur, armed with an automatic rifle, accompanied him. Slowly, they were approaching the factory entrance. But to his horror there was a gaping hole where once the hangar door had protected the cooling silo inside. Now there were remnants of wood, and shrieking noises coming from the belly of the factory.

It was almost impossible to walk against the wind and into the building. But, at last, Nightingale and his armed driver reached the two uniformed security men.

"They went that way," Bul yelled. "To the stairs."

Nineteen

The whole adventure finally revealed itself to them as one giant mistake. The blizzard blew in their faces with an unearthly force, and it was only because they knew there was no turning back, that they kept going. They were walking shoulder to shoulder with their heads down, their faces hidden in their furry parka hoods as much as possible; Zschopau in the middle, Pappas to his left and Sakamoto to his right. The bizz jockey and his producer were holding the arms of the old magician to give him some support, because by now it was clear that his strength was not coming from some endless source, but that it was human after all. That it was limited. It was all beginning to exhaust him, his knees growing weaker by the minute.

In addition to supporting their old comrade, Carl carried the valise under his left arm, and Hitomi carried the diskette box under her right arm.

They saw nothing, they heard nothing. The air was filled with snowflakes, flying horizontally as if they were trying to be on time for a secret rendez-vous in the distance. Probably the only good thing was that nobody on the Drenz premises would be foolhardy enough to follow their footsteps in the snow, or pick up their trail by sight or sound.

They were also lucky in another way: they walked to the forest in a straight line. It would have been easy for them to get lost, running in circles, but somehow they didn't, and within fifteen minutes they saw the dark shade of the forest shimmer through the relentless snowstorm. That renewed their strengths, and a few minutes later they arrived in the lee of the trees. The force of the wind and the snowflakes diminished quickly, until they passed the first trees and they were mostly out of the storm. So thick and wide were these woods, that there was only a mild wind, albeit still very cold, and an occasional flake. The howling of the wind was behind them now.

But the doctor was very weak and the cold was intense, their legs were shaky and they were unsure about the direction. In retrospect, this was a poorly prepared operation; there was no back-up plan and their route was a mere gamble. The doctor's white beard was turning him into a snowman, albeit hardly abominable.

===

Pappas, Sakamoto and Zschopau were not the only ones who had ventured to Drenz poorly prepared. William Nightingale felt exactly the same way.

How could I have come here without assistance? he wondered. How could I have come here being so naive? How could I have thought that Zschopau was going to quietly grow old and die and leave Z-mere at our mercy? How could I?

He was standing in the utility room, the men running around trying to find the renegades. But there wasn't a trace.

Nightingale hadn't been in this room, not in all the decades that he had visited this place. He didn't care about peripheral stuff, the utilities left him stone cold. But now... these burglars had been in here, and from what Bul and Jock had told him, an old man had been with them, and that could well have been Zschopau. Why else would an old man be in here? But it was the man and the woman that rounded it up for him: that could be no one else but the bizz jockey and his deceptively charming producer.

So it was perfectly clear what was going on here. But where could they have gone?

"There's nobody here," said Jock. "This place is empty. And your chauffeur is guarding the stairway, so they cannot go back up."

"There must be an exit," growled Nightingale, sounding like a wounded animal, making sounds that were in tune with the atonal howling of the storm above them. "Look closer. Listen, you"—he pointed to Jock—"check out this chamber again and again for a hidden exit. I'm going back up with your colleague to check the entire laboratory."

While he turned and walked to the corridor, it occurred to him that the giant cooling silo was not the only object that could be of interest to Zschopau. There was also the little vault where the original test results from the Doctor had been stored all these years. For safety reasons — with all the government spying going on since the "war on terror" it was unwise to store such delicate formulas on computers — it was kept there and there only. What if...

He started running.

===

As if the forest wasn't a dark enough place, night crawled upon them with sudden swiftness. Now they were relatively safe from the storm, but they weren't necessarily better off. They started stumbling over the branches and falling into small pits. Each time Carl and Hitomi had to literally pick up Zschopau from the ground.

Then, just as both the bizz jockey and his producer thought about what to do, how to deal with this, and how to break the news that they were in trouble, the doctor collapsed. His legs gave away, so his full weight was in their arms.

They all went down.

Carl cursed.

"Ernst!" yelled Hitomi.

Together they turned the limp body of The Great Mikado around. Hitomi got out her flashlight and shone at the doctor.

"Oh Carl, he's out," Hitomi said, her voice breaking. "What can we do?"

Carl looked on, dumbfounded.

Hitomi pointed the light at the bizz jockey.

"Carl, you're shaking, are you with me? Hey! Man, your lips are blue."

"I-I-I," stammered Pappas, "I'm cold, dammit. I'm sorry."

"We can't make a fire here," said Hitomi. "There's still too much wind."

"At l-l-least you're not..."

"Sssh..." said Hitomi. "Try to say something funny. You're

good at that, BJ. What's that you always say when things get bad?"

"Th-th-this is going to get a lot worse b-b-before it get's any better."

She thought frantically. Things were spinning out of control.

We need outside help, Hitomi thought. We need it and we need it fast.

Twenty

It had been a mean blizzard. But as they soon found out, things did not improve when it was over.

The wind, the snow, the clouds — they were all gone in less than an hour, making room for a starlit night. Even through the canopy of the pine trees they could see the stars up there, but they could see no beauty in it.

It was too cold for that now.

They had carried the lifeless body of Dr. Ernst Zschopau between them, and the old man's papers and floppy disks too, for a long way into the forest. But eventually Carl's legs gave up on him too and he had to stop.

He was shaking like a maniac and he was complaining about not feeling his toes and his fingers, and Hitomi knew his body temperature was dropping too fast. She was having trouble getting through to him, he seemed to be losing all his focus.

She sighed and looked up.

Then she started to unzip his parka, her own parka, remove stuff that was underneath his parka, stuff that was underneath her parka, and so forth, and eventually found a way to warm up the bizz jockey by bringing her sinewy body in direct contact with his. Feeling his coldness, she was at once determined to do anything within her power to rescue him. He was already losing consciousness, so it was time to take drastic measures. Her hands moved across the bizz jockey's body.

With a little luck, he won't remember any of this, she thought. And if he does, I will reprimand the hell out of him. Or quit my job.

Twenty-one

Carl Pappas heard an electronic sound. It was a beep. He could not determine its origin right away, but it had to be quite close. He was, however, surrounded by utter darkness.

"Who's there?" he asked. "What?"

Someone shook him. As a result he instinctively opened his eyes.

It was day. They were still in the forest. Hitomi Sakamoto was sitting next to him on the forest floor, one hand on the zipper of his parka, and her cell phone in the other.

"Hitomi? What..."

"Carl, good to have you back," said Hitomi, studying whatever was happening on her cell phone. "Help is on the way."

The bizz jockey made some jerky gestures and got up. "What happened?"

"You slept. Now, I have a location on my cell phone map. There's a place nearby where we'll be picked up, but we have to get going. And also..." She raised a finger.

There were sounds in the distance. There was no doubt about it: there were dogs barking. Not close, but dogs nonetheless.

When they were standing up, they realized they had to carry their dead friend. They looked at the scientist, and then at each other for a moment, a long reluctant look, but also a look of understanding, and then they bent over and got started.

The dogs were closing in on them. They could hear it.

"Do you... like... dogs?" Carl asked, panting for the heavy load they were carrying.

"Carl Evangelos Pappas," said Hitomi, "after all these years do you really have to ask me that?"

"I was... just... making conversation," said Carl. "But now that you mention it: I do remember Don bringing a puppy dog along to the studio once and you getting in to a complete fit and putting the both of them on the street on ground level in no time."

"I advise you to dislike dogs too," said Hitomi, "at this particular moment."

"Recommendation accepted. Do you think pets would make an interesting topic for The Boardroom? I mean, all these pets combined make a billion dollar industry. Food, medicine, toys, housing..."

"Why not? You can talk about pets on the show anytime, you can even have guests to join you. But not a single animal will be granted permission to enter the building. I am not going to be responsible for beasts. Dealing with your sound engineer is about all I can stand."

Carl chuckled. Even in the midst of this disaster, Hitomi Sakamoto didn't give an inch.

The remote sounds of the dogs behind them were becoming clearer.

They tried to run, but it was impossible. They couldn't manage anything else but a new kind of speed-stumbling. Tripping over yet another branch or the root of a tree, getting up as fast as they could and resuming their pace was about all they could muster.

"We're close now, Carl," said Hitomi, looking at her cell phone. On an app, a map of the area was visible, nothing more than the color of green, showing the uninhabited, roadless forest, with a blue pulse and a red dot.

The barking was ever so close now.

There was also another sound, a sound they didn't immediately recognize. But as they carried on, slowing down more and more, they realized it had to be a helicopter.

"Can they land that thing here?" shouted Carl, as the noise was becoming overwhelming, the roaring of the engine, the hissing sounds of air.

Then the sound no longer approached them, but came down. The helicopter was landing right in front of them. The rotors blew up snow, they could see the movement through the trees, the helicopter's hulk descending in a cloud.

It all gave them new energy. The hope of being taken away from this place, but also the fear that was induced by the sound of the dogs that could be heard beyond the thundering roar of the machine.

By the time they reached the clearing where their transport had landed, two men came running towards them with a stretcher and took over their heavy load. Behind them, partially hidden in clouds of snow, was a transport helicopter that had once belonged to some army, but was painted black now.

"Go, go, go!" one of the men barked.

Not only did he sound like a military from a movie, they both looked the part: white camouflage outfits, warm enough for an arctic winter, with protective glasses.

They were also in good shape, rushing back to the helicopter with great agility, plowing the snow and jumping the branches, not minding the powerful stream of air that came from the rotors, and the snow that was blown all around them.

Within moments, The Great Mikado was on board and Carl and Hitomi were aided climbing in.

From the forest the barking became louder and louder.

"Go!" barked the same team member.

The pilot shoved some handles and the helicopter started to climb fast. The hanging door was still open, and they could see dogs enter the clearing, confused by the snow blowing into their snouts. A man was holding both dogs on a leash, and two more men stepped from the trees.

Carl saw one man aim a rifle at them, and he drew Hitomi down with him, keeping her behind his body for protection.

One of the men on the ground grabbed the rifle and pushed it away, and a shot was fired into the snow.

"And we're out!" someone said.

"They're shooting!" yelled Hitomi.

"No," said Carl. "Not any more."

They stared at the blanket on the stretcher, and the old

man's shape, and forgot about the dangers. In the movements
and the noise, Pappas heard one of the men speak to the pilot,
saying something about "Mach" — which made perfect sense
to him.

Twenty-two

It's just another stupid idea, the random output of an idiot's mind, Carl Pappas thought.

He was looking straight into the deep hole, dug into the frozen soil, amidst mountains of snow. There was so much white breath in the frigid air that it was hard to look anyone in the eye.

But then this was not a moment to look anyone in the eye, so he looked down into Doctor Ernst Zschopau's grave, and started to wonder about how on earth they had been able to dig this hole in the solid soil.

Who cares? he thought. Stop thinking stupid things and remember Ernst Zschopau properly for a moment.

There were a lot of people at the funeral. Apparently The Great Mikado had been a local hero. The mayor was there, people from the police and fire departments, local newspapers and TV stations, as well as hundreds of others.

So there he stood, feeling sorry for the old man, who had indeed been one of the friendliest old geezers he'd ever met, willing to take some chances, and with a physical strength that was nothing less than unbelievable for anyone so ancient. It was at times like these that the bizz jockey thought about retiring. About walking away and looking for something completely different to do for a living.

Maybe I can become my girlfriend's secretary, he thought.

Then he shook himself out of this thinking mode, just in time to hear Hitomi say "Thank you".

There, you've missed Hitomi's speech, Carl thought. You're so full of it.

Hitomi took two steps back and stood next to her boss again. Carl felt her take his hand, even though they both wore the thickest gloves.

As he tried to look straight ahead without focusing on anything in particular — which is what one does at funerals a lot of the time — he stared right into the face of Mach One. The man was standing in the crowd, his floppy hat drawn way down over his eyes and his collar standing up pointing at his nose – but he was recognizable nonetheless.

Carl smiled for a moment. Not at Mach, but at himself and at the thought of Ernst Zschopau, and the crazy adventure with the old scientist and Hitomi. Had it been worth it? What had been achieved other than the death of a nice man?

Who wants to be a warrior for a better world if it means standing at a friend's grave in the freezing cold?

Then he saw Mach One smile for a second, before turning and disappearing instantaneously into the crowd.

They'd better get it over with and close this grave quickly, Carl thought, before this heap of sand is frozen solid again.

"Nice topic for a show," Hitomi whispered.

He looked at her silently and saw that her eyes were moist.

"What?"

"The funeral business," she said.

Somehow that was comforting: the beginning of a return to business as usual.

Twenty-three

"So we're all in this together, is that it Leandros?" said the bizz jockey, talking loud and clear into his trusted Shure SM7 microphone, addressing a faceless caller.

"Of course we are," a voice said in Carl Pappas' headphones, but also through the sound systems that were installed in the sound booth and both the editorial and visitors' rooms, all behind glass and all looking out into the space were The Boardroom was recorded and broadcast live. "The state of the worldwide debts is nobody's fault and it is also everybody's fault. I'd say quit talking, roll up your sleeves. There's work to be done."

"Hush, Leandros, I agree with that last remark, yes, there's work to be done. But if you think I'm going along with that nobody-is-to-blame-and-we're-all-guilty crap, you are dead wrong. You're a bad boy. Go do your homework again. Lehman didn't fall because of the ordinary man, but because bankers were dealing in toxic packages."

"Home-owners were also to blame for that!"

"Oh come on, Leandros. You are in the wrong camp, I can smell you people from a mile away. If you offer people a mortgage they can't afford, fine, you can say you're a clever businessman. But the point is, you are responsible as a banker because you have the opportunity. Bankers who deal in toxic stuff, are responsible because they are in a position to know what they're doing. Ordinary folk are not. And where is it written that if everybody's as guilty as you are, you are suddenly relieved of responsibility? Shame on you, Leandros. Pointing your finger at little people. We are talking about you here. Call me again if you have a valid argument for a change!"

He made his trademark cutthroat gesture with his index finger and sat back, jerking off his headphones. Beyond the window, Don Wozniak opened a gate and soft piano music flooded from the sound system.

Phil Solo walked in. "I talked to Nightingale, Carl."

The bizz jockey sighed. "I'm not entirely sure if I want to know what's next."

"Told him to back off," said Solo, without a trace of his usual sarcasm. "His secrets are with us now. The future of Z-mere and its possible toxic side effects are no longer in his hands alone, or in the hands of his accomplices."

"You think he has a copy of Zschopau's formulas?"

"Seems likely. On computers somewhere else. Though he made quite a scene. Demanded to have Zschopau's papers back, and the diskettes."

"You didn't tell him the government has them now? He has been bribing people there for years."

"I told him nothing he doesn't need to know right now," said Phil. "I did convince him to sit still now, like a good dog. Anyhow, the government will deal with this. We're out of the loop, our lawyers like it that way. It's just..."

Pappas got up from behind the large studio table. "Let's have it, Phil. After all this, I'm like a rock again. Hit me with it!"

"I will not apologize for shouting abuse at your little burglary," said the WCBN Radio managing director. "I draw the line there. You are a radio man, an investigative reporter basically, a host. You let other people do the dirty work. If something happens to you, all these people who work for you, who adore you, are going to be left behind. You have ten million listeners. Who are you helping by acting like an irresponsible lunatic?"

And when the bizz jockey didn't respond, he added: "Huh?"

"These people are sitting on a pile of potential acid that could to immense damage in the future," snarled Carl, "and they are treating these acids like assets. Lucrative assets. I resent that."

After a moment of silence, Phil resumed. "Oh, well, I've made my point. Forget it. The government's on it, they're better equipped, and they're supposed to be handling this by law. I can't control you and I resent that, but I guess that's how it should be. I just want you to know that I just did the stupidest thing of my whole career."

Pappas smiled.

"I promised the government you would not mention any of this on live radio."

Then Phil Solo turned and left the room in a hurry, while behind him Carl yelled: "YOU DID WHAT?"

Don's voice came from the speakers: "That was funny,

Carl."

"Yeah, I guess."

"Another broken promise," said Don.

"I don't know," said the bizz jockey. "I'm not proud. One of the nicest old men I ever met in my life is dead and I have something to do with that."

"I understand he was at the end of his life anyhow..."

"Let's leave well enough alone, OK?"

The break was over. Commercials had come and gone and in those few minutes Carl Pappas had felt his mood sink further. From behind the glass, Hitomi Sakamoto had given him a gesture with a fist. In her body language that meant "hang in there", and it was at that moment that he knew how to honor Dr. Ernst Zschopau, The Great Mikado.

"I have no doubt some of you folks have known the refugee scientist, Dr. Ernst Zschopau," were his first words after the break.

He saw Hitomi nod softly.

"I have had the honor to meet him once," said Carl. "It was unforgettable. I apologize to all of you people who will think I am talking in riddles, but you have to trust me on this one: it serves a very humane purpose. If any of you folks know where Dr. Zschopau got his nickname The Great Mikado, I want you to hit that button on your radio app or hit Bizz Jockey on Google and find our number and call now."

And indeed, before the song that Don Wozniak played for a moment had finished, a caller was connected.

"I'd rather not say my name, if that's OK with you, Mr. Pappas," an old woman's voice sounded.

"You go right ahead, ma'am."

"For Ernst, mikado referred to the process of everything falling apart. That was how he approached his life when we were living in a totalitarian state a long time ago: even if bad things happened, they were part of the magical mikado, these loose wooden sticks that need to be picked up carefully so as not to disturb the others. A man has to recollect pieces and begin again, he thought. Always."

"Well how about that," said the bizz jockey, apparently at a loss for further words.

"Have you ever played with mikado, Mr. Pappas," asked the unknown woman.

Pappas heard Hitomi's voice in his earphones, a facility that was usually only used by the sound engineer.

"Many times," she said. "Many, many times."

"Many times, ma'am," the bizz jockey repeated after Hitomi, into the microphone. "It's a thing Dr. Zschopau and I had sort of in common. Create chaos and then have your pick."

•••

[1] During the Cold War, the Iron Curtain divided Europe into the free west and the communist east. This ideological and physical barrier came into existence in the years after the end of the Second World War in 1945 and climaxed after the raising of the Berlin Wall. With the collapse of communism, the Iron Curtain disappeared through 1989-1990.

[2] Predicted by scientists in the 1980s, great areas of floating garbage in the oceans have emerged in the early 21st century. They are not really islands, but areas where tiny fragments of plastics float under the ocean's surface, brought and kept there by the currents. Ships navigate around these areas as much as they can.

[3] Jozef Stalin (1878-1953) was a dictator who ruled over the Soviet Union until his death. Although he turned a largely backwards and agrarian nation into an industrialized world power in an extremely short time (compared to the industrialized West), and helped the Allies in the war against Germany and Japan, he is mainly remembered for being one of the most ruthless rulers in history; tens of millions of people died during his dictatorship.

[4] Aleksandr Solzhenitsyn (1918-2008) was an eminent

Russian novelist and critic of totalitarianism. He raised global awareness of the Soviet Union's forced labor camp system in books like "The Gulag Archipelago". GULAG is the acronym for "Chief Administration of Corrective Labor Camps and Colonies", its camps spread like islands across the vast emptiness of Siberia and other parts of the former USSR.

Request from the author

Thank you for reading this novel. I hope you enjoyed it and will be willing to write a review on the online platform of your choice. Making that extra effort is greatly appreciated by other readers... and of course by me. Thank you.

I hope you and I stay connected through Twitter, Facebook, Google+, Pinterest or my free email newsletter. I'll make sure you'll stay tuned.

Have a good evening/night/day!

M.H. Vesseur

Twitter @MHVesseur

Facebook www.facebook.com/MHVesseur

Subscribe to M.H. Vesseur's mailing list on www.mhvesseur.com

About the author

M.H. Vesseur has written many short stories for literary magazines in The Netherlands, Belgium, Canada and the U.S.A. He was awarded for the best debut with his first story. In his radio detective series about Carl Pappas he has now written and published the seven short crime novels *CEO Groupie*, *Die Rich*, *Tax Me If You Can*, *Acid Asset*, *Nosedive*, *Power Play* and *Blood Border*. The radio detective's producer Hitomi Sakamoto now stars in her own series, which begins with *North*. M.H. Vesseur also published the novel *Lemniscate*, a collection of literary short stories called *Allusions* and his outlook on the super economy *Burning Neil Armstrong*. M.H. Vesseur is an awarded advertising copywriter. He lives in the forests of The Netherlands.

www.mhvesseur.com

Novels and ebooks by M.H. Vesseur

More information on:
www.mhvesseur.com/publications

Allusions (short story collection)
North (The Hitomi Files: 1)
Blood Border (a Radio Detective novel)
Power Play (a Radio Detective novel)
Nosedive (a Radio Detective novel)
Acid Asset (a Radio Detective novel)
Tax Me If You Can (a Radio Detective novel)
Die Rich (a Radio Detective novel)
CEO Groupie (a Radio Detective novel)
Beloved Stalker
Babyface Junkie
In Snuff Park
Sketches Of A Worldwide Christo And Jeanne-Claude
Narcissist Guru
Territory Game

Short stories by M.H. Vesseur

ALLUSIONS

Glimpses of tomorrow await you in this collection. The ultimate amusement park will offer you death. Everlasting youth will take you to the point of no return. The artificial landscape will fill you with joy if it doesn't scare the living daylights out of you. The Narcissist Guru will show you your many selves. There is the ultimate work of art that will change the planet and the old vaudeville star who is still being stalked. And finally, the coming of the super economy will haunt your dreams. This collection contains the short stories • In Snuff Park • Babyface Junkie • Narcissist Guru • Sketches of a Worldwide Christo and Jeanne-Claude • Territory Game • Beloved Stalker • Burning Neil Armstrong.

Available in The Hitomi Files by M.H. Vesseur

NORTH

Man should fear only one enemy

The only enemy who has the capacity to remove all of mankind from the earth, is the virus. Imagine the worst of them all, a true 21st century killer. It lies dormant in the remote laboratory of a pharmaceutical giant whose hopes of making billions off a vaccine somewhere in the future throw a dark shadow ahead. Then Hitomi Sakamoto, the hard boiled radio producer who's on a rough vacation in the wild nature of the north, stumbles upon this dark secret. She is drawn into a final battle between ruthless scientists, a greedy corporation, desperate but dangerous environmental activists, a cold-hearted assassin and... a manmade virus that longs to escape.

Hitomi Sakamoto first appeared in the Radio Detective novels by

M.H. Vesseur. Immediately popular for her iron work ethics and razorsharp tongue, Hitomi outgrew her boss (radio detective Carl Pappas) and now steps out of his shadow, into her very own adventure.

Available in the radio detective series by M.H. Vesseur

CEO GROUPIE - A radio detective novel

One night three live guests join Carl Pappas on his radio show The Boardroom: two CEOs and a woman who calls herself: "the CEO Groupie". When the mysterious woman reveals the existence of a secret call girl organization for CEOs and subsequently disappears a couple of days later, the bizz jockey engages on a search. What happened to the CEO Groupie and what are the other two guests up to? Together with his radio team — his producer Hitomi Sakamoto and his sound engineer Don Wozniak — Carl Pappas sets out to deal with this.

Available in the radio detective series by M.H. Vesseur

DIE RICH - A radio detective novel

Carl Pappas, the bizz jockey, goes on the air again. His radio show "The Boardroom" is both loved and feared by the global business community. He has a sharp eye for business news and the big mouth of a talk radio host. This time around he has some very wealthy guests joining him on his show: two billionaire entrepeneurs and their future successors, who also happen to be their sons. Of course it doesn't take the bizz jockey a very long time to upset some of his guests and his audience — and that same night the bizz jockey finds himself heading into dangerous waters, in the hands of some very angry rich people. His team — producer Hitomi Sakamoto and sound engineer Don Wozniak — is forced to go out and rescue their reckless boss. And then there are the rich kids they have to deal with...

Available in the radio detective series by M.H. Vesseur

TAX ME IF YOU CAN - A radio detective novel

Carl Pappas, the bizz jockey, is cooking up a real shocker: during a live broadcast of his popular business talk radio show "The Boardroom" he plans to reveal secrets about tax dodging practices around the globe. In the middle of the preparations he and his producer Hitomi Sakamoto face unexpected trouble. Who is trying to shut the Bizz Jockey up in this quiet country under the tropical sun? Is it the local military junta? Is it the business community? Or is the sun finally getting to Carl Pappas' head?

Also available in the radio detective series

NOSEDIVE - A radio detective novel

When a large corporation is struck by a cripling strike among its workers and an apparent terrorist attack on its factory, bizz jockey Carl Pappas steps forward to offer his public support. But as he soon finds out, there's more to the picture than meets the eye. Why is the owner hiding in her large mansion? What happened in her youth that is threatening her after all these years? It's a job for the radio detective — and this time around his boss gives an unexpected hand.

Available in the radio detective series by M.H. Vesseur

BLOOD BORDER - A radio detective novel

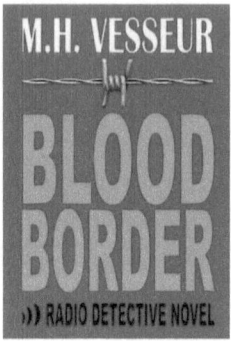

The inhumanity of human trafficking is forcing the radio detective to make a stand. So in the midst of politics and public outrage, Carl Pappas and his team infiltrate the trafficking cartel of a man known as The Clown. But there is nothing funny about it, for the radio detective soon finds himself in the lion's den, a place crowded with former narcotics traffickers and their violent ways. Will they be able to do something about the screaming injustice of immigration or will they become prey themselves?

<<<<>>>>